FIRST BLOOD

Charley Fever stepped into something slippery and nearly lost his footing. Then the odor hit him, and he knew that he was standing in human blood.

"It's Tommy Noble and Harry the Gook," the kid explained through stiffened lips. "Don't look, Mr. Fever. Most of their heads are gone."

"Well, shit," Fever said softly. Then he retraced his steps across the messy porch and wiped the blood from his shoes.

This was *first* blood, he was thinking. But a hell of a long ways—bet on that—from the *last*.

For damn sure, deadeye Bolan had been there that night. Yeah. And the hell was just starting.

The bestselling adventure series in the country!

The Executioner

And more to come . . .

THE
EXECUTIONER

DETROIT DEATHWATCH

by
Don Pendleton

PINNACLE BOOKS • NEW YORK CITY

Dedicated with admiration
to all those who patrol the jungle
yet remain immune to the dehumanizing
influences there. Stay hard.

DETROIT DEATHWATCH

Copyright © 1974 by Pinnacle Books, Inc.

An original Pinnacle Books edition, published for the
first time anywhere.

ISBN: 0-523-00419-2

First printing, June 1974

Printed in the United States of America

PINNACLE BOOKS, INC.
275 Madison Avenue
New York, N.Y. 10016

Of all the benefits
which virtue confers on us,
the contempt of death
is one of the greatest.
                    —Michel de Montaigne

Death is watching me.
I am watching her back.
It is a game
at which two can play.
                    —Mack Bolan, the Executioner

PROLOGUE

Mack Bolan had never thought that he would live forever. He had not really expected to survive even the first pitched battle of his war against the Mafia.

A military realist, Bolan had been strongly aware from the very beginning that he was waging a war of hopeless dimensions. Even so, he was not a *banzai* soldier. Suicide had no part in this soldier's thinking. He was a cool strategist and a masterful tactician. His war was planned and fought with military precision, directed toward specific goals and calculated effects. One overriding consideration was, of course, to *remain alive* and, by extension, to keep his war alive. Not a cold war but a very hot one—*blitzkrieg*, thunder and lightning, death and destruction, shattered flesh and flowing blood, fear, panic, hysteria—all were Bolan's stock in trade, and he meant to keep that stock active for as long as possible.

Not, however, in the name of vengeance. Revenge could move a man just so far—and Bolan had long ago passed that limitation of vengeful motivation. Granted, his first reflexive action against the mob had been primarily motivated by a need to strike back, to achieve justice in the only clear manner available. The mob had been responsible for the violent deaths of Mom and Pop Bolan and kid sister Cindy. Police officials in the home town of Pittsfield had admitted their own helplessness in the matter. This professional soldier had not felt helpless. He was a trained death machine, an expert in one-man warfare. He had earned his code name, the "Executioner," through repeated successful penetrations into enemy enclaves in Vietnam and had been credited with 95 official "kills" of enemy VIPs. He had been described by superiors as "nerveless"; by army psychologists as "self-commanding"; and by the enemy command as "that devil." Sergeant Bolan was perhaps the first noncom in American history to carry an enemy pricetag on his head.

So, no, Bolan had not felt helpless in dealing with those responsible for his personal family tragedy. He quickly "executed" five of those most directly responsible and immediately set out to track down the sixth. It was not until this point that he learned the identity of this "new enemy" —"the Mafia, for God's sake!"—the fabled crime organization that a Senate investigator had labeled "the invisible second government of the nation."

Bolan did not dig that kind of "government." It quickly became apparent to this professional soldier that the Mafia posed the gravest threat ever encountered by his country. His feeling in this regard is revealed by an entry in his personal journal, penned in the early days of his Mafia war: "Why defend a front line 8,000 miles away when the *real* enemy is chewing up everything you love back home?"

Being human, Bolan was not immune to the scare stories concerning the Mafia's power and ruthlessness—and, yes, he was decidedly uneasy about "taking on the whole damn Mafia." He knew that an organization that had built its success upon fear and intimidation could not turn its back on this counterattack, even by a single individual. An act of violence upon any *mafioso* would be regarded as an attack upon the entire organization —a debt of honor to be expunged quickly and decisively—and, in the beginning, Bolan knew that he was little more than a flea upon the back of the giant Mafia dog. He resolved, however, to be as pesky as possible for as much time as he had left —to "bring thunder and lightning to their house!" In such terms did Bolan declare the one-man war to the death against an almost omnipotent enemy —and thus began the most stirring and heroic human commitment in modern history.

With that first unexpected victory at Pittsfield came a closer understanding of the enemy and a deepening of the commitment. Bolan sallied forth then to slay the Mafia dragon wherever contact could be made—and those contacts became legion.

The personal hazards were compounded, also. He was operating outside the law and counter to every moral precept of his society. His name became prominent on the wanted lists of police establishments throughout the country and eventually around the world. Besides quickening police interest, Bolan had to contend also with hordes of free-lance gunmen, bounty hunters who hoped to cash in on the $100,000 "open contract" set by the Mafia ganglords.

As the impossible odds against survival thus pyramided, the man himself "grew into" the situation—sharpened by the challenges, refined by constant peril, enlarged by each confrontation with almost certain death, strengthened by each piecemeal victory.

Bolan, the man, was not, however, all guts and gore. There existed a sensitive human dimension to the warrior that was evident as far back as the researcher cares to delve. While he was being lauded as the "Executioner" in the hellgrounds of Vietnam, other contemporaries quietly referred to the man as "Sergeant Mercy," in recognition of his selfless services to the civilian victims of that war. Friends and associates of earlier times characterized the youthful Bolan as kind and sincerely idealistic, a thoughtful young man who seemed to be guided by a deep sense of human ethics and compassion.

That these same attributes accompanied the man into his impossible war seems borne out by the attitude of many lawmen and other close observers who secretly cheered him on and sometimes openly offered him aid and comfort. A comrade summed up the Bolan paradox with the words: "It's a weird combination of tough guts and warm heart. Most men wouldn't know how to carry both together. The sarge does."

Bolan's closest friend and only continuing ally was an undercover federal agent who had attained high rank in one of the Mafia families. No matter how desperate his situation, Bolan had never been known to fire upon a lawman, and many times he had risked his own capture or death to protect these "soldiers of the same side."

In many quarters of his society, Bolan had become a folk hero. The press was generally sympathetic to the man and his mission, though there were those who frequently denounced his methods and editorialized for his early capture. There were some in government who thought that Mack Bolan should be regarded as a national hero, and indeed there had been aborted attempts to extend an offer of amnesty plus official status in the government's own war against organized crime.

Through it all, the man walked his own path, mostly alone, a "free agent" in his own mind. Autonomous, self-propelled, selecting his own missions and carrying them through to his own idea of a proper conclusion, marked for death and accepting this as a proper judgment, he gave his every energy to a delay of that sentence, realizing that in this war of attrition, his side was allowed but one casualty.

He could not, of course, live forever. No one knew this better than the man himself. He had learned to take life by the heartbeat, one at a time. This was, in his own understanding, "living large."

Survival itself, however, held no meaning except in the sense that it was advancing his cause, his war. In this understanding, Bolan lived only to kill. But to kill in such a manner that he himself might live on to kill again and again. To paraphrase a childhood epigram, he lived to kill and killed to live. This would seem a shabby pretext for life if viewed entirely upon the surface of the man's war. The man himself had deeper dimensions, however, and he took very seriously this violent destiny that had made of his entire life a jungle. He knew the rules here. He accepted the penalties. And he played the game to win.

It was perhaps for this latter consideration that Bolan had thus far avoided the city that was known to be the home of "the most stable crime family in the nation." The risks there were too great, the odds too impossible, the task too complex to even formulate a coherent goal of combat. But the Executioner had avoided Detroit for as long as he could. Much as any man would turn with a sigh to face his own inevitable destruction, the mighty Bolan turned to Detroit to face the challenge that he had always known awaited him there. Others turned with him, expectantly, confidently, certain that this would be the final battle of the Executioner Wars and eager to be in on the deathwatch.

No, Mack Bolan had never expected to live forever. But, sure, he played the game to win. He had come to Detroit not to die but to make war. "This whole town is a hardsite," he wrote in his journal on the eve of the Detroit bloodletting. "So let's take it one heartbeat at a time, on the numbers. If this has to be the final battle, so be it. Let's just make it worthy of the name."

Executioner Bolan was taking on the economic heartland of the nation, and for a very good reason. That heartland was a "hardsite"—an armed camp, a fortress of Mafia power—and the nation was coming into hard times. Cancer thrives on a weakened body—Bolan knew that. A powerful Mafia concentration at the hub of American industry, at such a time, could have nothing but disastrous consequences for the country as a whole. And he knew that he had to break that death grip . . . or he had to die trying.

So, yes, Bolan turned to Detroit with a determined sigh. And the city turned to *the Executioner,* herself sighing into the deathwatch, knowing full well that *judgment* had come to the *Ville d'Etroit*—the City of the Strait. She would become the City of the *Straight*—or she, too, would die in the attempt.

Resurget Cineribus—It Shall Rise Again from the Ashes—had been the motto for this old city since the great fire of 1805, along with *Speramus Meliora*—We Hope for Better Things. Bolan understood and sympathized with both ideas—but he knew that a soldier did not rise again from his own ashes—and he had long ago given up on mere "hope."

A man *fought* for better things.

And sometimes, he *died* for them.

7

1: TARGETED

The watcher was being watched, and he knew it.

But, yeah, that was okay. It was what he wanted, expected.

He was standing a few hundred yards offshore, riding at sea anchor, getting the feel of the big twenty-power nightscope, as the tethered cruiser bobbed gently and rhythmically with the feeble undulations of Lake St. Clair. A scattering of shoreside estates glittered at him across the water, bright lights reflecting off the lake and adding an artificial luminescence to the atmosphere.

One of these in particular held his full attention.

And, sure, their security was pretty good. He had probably been spotted the moment he reached target range, and watched with mounting interest thereafter.

But he had the vision advantage, for two well-calculated reasons. The *Startron* scope was the chief advantage. It amplified scattered light rays and bent them into the optics with the effect of greatly heightened night vision—very much like that of a jungle cat, Bolan supposed.

The second advantage was provided by the night itself. The moon was full, low, behind him. There were no clouds. The wind was slanting in toward shore from the northeast, also at his back —not strong enough to affect targeting but enough to water the eyes a bit when staring straight into it, as was required of those watchers on the shore.

They could probably see no more than the black silhouette of a cabin cruiser anchored offshore, and perhaps the darkened figure of a man seated motionless on the flying bridge. Even it they'd had the advantage of night optics, chances were about even that the thing in his arms would be taken for a fishing rod.

Bolan was betting his life that they did not have night optics. And the thing in his arms was no fishing rod. It was the favored Mark V Weatherby—a hefty piece with a tripod swivel mount—based at a comfortable distance from the elevated fishing chair.

He was strapped into the rig in such a way that man and weapon were one with the gentle motions of the boat, and he was "feeling in" the rhythmical target-displacement produced by that motion, learning to compensate and keep his target centered, using this same exercise as an opportunity to evaluate the situation in the target zone.

It was a big joint, two stories, a lot of glass fronting the lakeshore—large porch, wide cement steps to the lawn, well-lighted grounds. A circular drive wound in from the far side, only partially visible beyond the corners of the house, but those areas showing evidence of many parked vehicles.

Hardmen were spotted about the grounds—most of whom were now gazing lakeward, grim-faced, wondering—no doubt intrigued by the possibilities presented by the presence of the intruder out there. Two were trotting along the pier, hurrying toward an outboard motorboat—a boarding party, no doubt.

And now the lights were going off in the house. Two hard-looking guys in nautical togs and yachting caps stepped outside to take up stations at the top of the steps.

Sure. Very cautious. Taking no chances.

And with good reason. Things had been getting tense in Detroit. There were rumors of armed clashes between the Combination and some of its franchised gangs, most notably the blacks. Coupled with this, the feds had been doing a lot of harassing lately, with around-the-clock surveillance, phone taps, occasional minor busts.

And now there was this boat, anchored just offshore . . .

Sure, they were being careful. And they did not know, yet, that the Executioner was stalking them, as well.

But they were going to know. And damn soon.

With a small sigh, Bolan lifted off of the eye-piece, double-checked his range calibrations, took a last look at the wind indicator, then leaned back into the scope and pitched his combat-consciousness into the final evaluation.

The crosshairs tracked the lakefront from north

to south, then began a methodical sectioning and cross-sectioning toward the house.

He heard the cough and sputter of an outboard motor being coaxed to life; ignored it; hung stubbornly to the eyepiece of the *Startron* as the gridding operation developed and formed into a coherent plan of attack; then froze and hung in a sort of suspended animation as target one swung into the hairs—a little medallion with crossed anchors affixed to a jauntily worn yachting cap.

He squeezed into the target, riding expertly with the recoil and grimacing to maintain optic continuity, grunting with professional satisfaction as the two-inch target disintegrated into a background of exploding red and white.

Trajectory evaluation: Perfect, point-blank. No correction required.

The targets themselves were correcting, however. The big 300-grain chunk of sizzling steel beat the sound wave by a couple of seconds. The headless hardman had pitched backwards and hit the cement porch at the precise instant that the powerful *cra-ack* of the big piece explained why —sending people in motion everywhere over there.

Bolan's crosshairs picked up the second yachting cap about halfway down the steps; another screaming .460 punched it into the air, and the man beneath flopped grotesquely and rolled to the bottom of the steps.

The next two rounds went deliberately high to shatter plate glass and wreak havoc on the interior. The remaining lights in there were quickly extinguished. The swivel moved on to the next preselected grid. A target there ran through the hairs and picked up track. Conditioned reflexes sighed into the squeeze. Round 5 sizzled along its flat ballistics course to overtake and overcome mere flesh, and another errant soul was returned to the universe.

Bolan lifted off, jaw tense, eyes iced.

Situation evaluation: Great. The delayed reaction was coming now, in the form of return-fire from several quarters. Two dudes on the roof, with rifles. Several near the water, in a trench or something. Others closing to center from both ends of the lakeshore. Some advancing along the lawn in front of the house.

The riflemen were having trouble ranging him, though, and he had counted on that. A silhouette on water, with a bright moon in the background, could be very deceptive. The first scattered fusillades were coming in low, falling short. They'd be finding their range very quickly, of course—and Bolan was now moving on tight numbers.

The motorboat had closed about half the distance. Those aboard apparently had nothing better than handguns and were waiting for a closer shot. Bolan tuned his hairs to that problem and quickly solved it with two heavy rounds smashing in at the waterline and a third punching into the motor. The boat immediately lost headway, and its two occupants went into a hasty abandon-ship drill.

Bolan smiled grimly and retreated below, taking the Weatherby with him. He carefully stowed the impressive piece in a watertight float bag, then he went forward and quickly hauled in the sea anchor.

His craft was taking repeated hits now, in a manner that could not suggest blind luck on the other end.

So, okay, he was ready.

He started the engine and kicked in full throttle, pulling away in a roaring circle toward open water, then brought her around to the desired course and secured the steerage on that heading.

An instant later he slipped over the side and began quietly working his way landward, while the cruiser plunged on toward Ontario.

The rifle fire from the shore was dying out, replaced now by the full-throated roar of a powerful cruiser that was leaping into hot pursuit of Bolan's abandoned boat.

He was within earshot when the big speedster paused to pick up the survivors from the outboard. He listened with interest to the angry mouthings and profane promises of the chase. And he was grinning to himself as they sped off into the night.

There were easily a dozen men aboard that craft, which meant that most of the hard force were now chasing an empty boat out across the wide reaches of Lake St. Clair.

Which was, of course, precisely what the Executioner had hoped for.

He hooked an arm into the flotation bag, oriented himself to the big joint on the shore, and continued on.

The real target of the night lay at the end of a five-minute swim.

The assault on Fortress Detroit was underway.

2: BLOODIED

The place on Grosse Pointe Shores had once been the lakeside estate of a pioneer auto magnate. It had been purchased by the Combination some years back, remodeled a bit, and christened "The Sons of Columbus Yacht Club." There was not, of course, a genuine yachtsman on the roster. The original idea had been to provide a genteel and exclusive resort for the families of the lower echelon *mafiosi* of the area, a sort of club for employees. The new charter also provided an excellent conduit for the washing of black money, and served as a nice cover for secret meetings and various illicit activities such as gambling, prostitution, smuggling, and so on—so much so that most of the members stopped bringing their families around, in deference to the other, more meaningful, activities. Eventually the SCYC was placed off-limits to the sons and daughters and wives, and was operated strictly as a mob headquarters.

Now the Combination entertained their friends and future friends here, consummated business deals, and held "family" councils and other secret rites, such as initiations and executions.

The location could not have been more convenient, nor, certainly, more exclusive from a social standpoint. Most everybody who was anybody in metropolitan Detroit lived within a ten-minute drive to the "club"—and, indeed, the entire ruling council of the Detroit Combination lived within walking distance. Even a special visitor from Windsor could hot it across the Ambassador Bridge and zoom out the Edsel Ford Freeway in less than a thirty-minute trip. For those who felt a bit shy about presenting themselves through U.S. Customs, there was always the Detroit River and Lake St. Clair—with an innocent and entirely legitimate yacht club ready to receive these special visitors at all hours.

On this particular evening, the SCYC was the chosen site for an "area conference." Important men from both sides of the border had been invited to attend. A few had flown in from as far away as Toronto and Buffalo.

It was to be an important meeting. First of all, of course, was the issue that was on everyone's mind these days: the "energy crunch" and how it could be turned to the best interests of the Detroit Combination. Of almost equal interest were the unsettling developments down Texas way. Many millions of Detroit-area dollars had been invested in the Flag Seven gamble, and the dust was just beginning to settle around Texas in the wake of that Bolan bastard. The question on everyone's mind, of course, was how much had been lost and how much could they reasonably expect to recoup.

With regard to this latter problem, nothing had been said beyond the usual condolences directed to Anthony Quaso, who had lost his kid brother in Bolan's latest blitz.

Quaso was high in the administration of Salvatore (Crazy Sal) Vincenti, one of the top bosses in Detroit. They had just buried young Joe Quaso a few days earlier, and this meeting was the first opportunity for many of those present to personally express their sympathy.

The talk had then inevitably turned to the "Bolan problem." A nervous industrialist from Toronto had voiced the fear that the "direct Quaso link to Texas" would magnetically attract Mack Bolan to the Detroit operations.

Sal Vincenti had scoffed at that suggestion, assuring one and all that "the guy wouldn't dare show his tail around here."

And then the house chief of security had come in to quietly advise Mr. Vincenti of the presence of a strange boat anchored just offshore.

"Send someone over to check it out," Vincenti instructed the house boss. Then he'd tried to get the conference back into the mainstream discussion, but somehow nothing really jelled after that. And this made Charley Fever nervous.

Charley Fever (born Favorini) was Sal Vincenti's chief torpedo—the one Vincenti himself often referred to as "my good third arm." That good arm had been seated directly behind his boss throughout the meeting, more like a brooding ghost who was there but not really, present for the proceedings but really not part of them. Vincenti was the only boss in the Combination who could get away with bringing his personal triggerman into the conference rooms—primarily because Crazy Sal was the uncrowned but actual boss of the works, partly also because the other bosses genuinely respected and trusted Charley Fever—more so than they trusted Crazy Sal.

Vincenti was given to ungovernable rages, sometimes over trifling or imagined offenses. Charley Fever was a godsend at such times. He had a special knack for calming his boss and defusing the emotional tizzies—or heading them off.

At this paricular point in the evening's proceedings, Charley had moved to the edge of his chair and was watching the old man like a hawk. All it took to get a collection of "friends" nervous and jumpy was to mention the name *Bolan*. And when the friends got jumpy, someone might say the wrong thing to Sal Vincenti, and then look out. Charley Fever was already looking out.

Then the shooting started. Everyone stood up and stared solemnly at the shuttered windows. Without a word, Charley glided over and took Vincenti by the arm, and they walked together to the "strong room"—a specially fortified chamber that was designed for just such emergencies. The others followed in single file, quietly, no pushing or shoving, as meek as schoolchildren going through the rote of a fire drill.

Charley Fever left them there and quickly went downstairs, extinguishing lights en route and calling out instructions to the house guard.

A breathless messenger met him at the first

landing and reported the happenings outside. Charley sent the guy on up to carry the news to the top, then he descended to the glass-littered mess below.

Some nut in a boat . . . getting his jollies with a high-powered rifle. That was how it sounded. It wouldn't be Black Johnson's niggers . . . not this way. But it was no time for snap judgments, and the security of a joint such as this one was not based on that kind of thinking.

Actually, Charley Fever had no direct interest in the security at SCYC. The joint ran itself, with its own force and its own honchos; but Charley Fever was responsible for the skin of old man Vincenti, and there was no way to restrict the authority of that position. He found the housekeeper and gave him instructions for the staff, then he went through the clubroom and across the darkened threshold to the porch.

The shooting had stopped. The house boss, a skinny veteran named Billy Castelano, was standing stiffly near the steps, peering down at something in the darkness below.

Charley Fever stepped into something slippery and nearly lost his footing—then the odor hit him, and he knew that he was standing in human blood. Only then did he notice the crumpled form lying off to the side, less than a pace away.

"What the hell . . . !" he exclaimed.

"It's Tommy Noble and Harry the Gook," Castelano explained through stiffened lips. "Don't look, Mr. Fever. Most of their head is gone."

"They got it in the *head?*" Charley Fever muttered. "*Both* of them?"

"Yessir. Whoever it was sure knows how to shoot. And he must know it. To go for the head, from way out there . . ."

"How far out there, Billy?"

"Far enough that these boys never knew what hit them. They was dead before the sound got here."

"I didn't know anybody had got hit," the chief torpedo said, his voice subdued. "I thought it was just . . ." The voice got lost in the machinery of thought, then returned with ". . . in the *head*, uh?"

At that moment the yard boss materialized from the shadows of the lawn to call up, "Maybe you better go back inside! We don't know what the hell is going on here, yet!"

Castelano jerked about and retreated across the porch, but Fever held his position to call back, "What's it look like, Mickey?"

"Hell, I dunno," the yard chief replied. "All the incoming was from a boat." He moved a couple of paces closer to add, "They turned tail and ran before we even got set. Joe and his boys are chasing them out on the lake. Don't worry, nothing can outrun the *Chris Columbus*. He'll catch the bastards."

"How many bastards you figure?"

"God, I don't know that, Mr. Fever. They only fired about seven or eight rounds. Some of those were at the gig. Sunk it. Tony Dollar and Pete Dominic were on their way out when the shooting started. They're okay, I guess. I saw Joe stop and pick them up."

"How many dead men we got around here, then?" Charley Fever wondered aloud.

"Three, sir. I guess you saw Tom and Harry. Also this new guy from the old country, this Roccobello kid."

"He get it in the head?" Charley Fever asked quietly.

"Yessir. They all did."

"Yeah, they all did," the boss torpedo echoed, his voice soft and curiously flattened. He joined Castelano at the door and pulled him inside. "Go upstairs and tell Sal I said he should stay in the strong room until he hears from me. Also, he should call his legal eagles, get them out here quick. Cops'll be swarming in here soon, you can bet on that, and maybe even those fancy feds will take the excuse to horn in."

"Hell, we're a legit security outfit, sir," Castelano protested. "We got a right to defend the joint."

"Sure you have," Charley Fever replied smoothly. "But the cops also have a legit right to investigate any shootings, so you scoot and tell Sal. We don't want the bosses and their friends subjected to that crap, do we?"

"Right. I'll get the cars over on the quiet exit, too. Some of these *amici* won't want to be around here when the bulls arrive. Check, sir, I'll take care of the details."

"Do that," Charley Fever said with a thin smile. He watched the house boss hustle away, then he turned to his own thoughts.

Charley Fever had heard every one of those incoming shots. They all came from the same gun, and a hell of a big one. But *one* gun. That meant one *gunner*. And three good boys shot squarely through the head—dead before the bodies dropped —dead before they even heard the shot that killed them.

That took some damned good shooting.

At nighttime, yet.

Sure, it sounded just like . . .

He lit a cigar, then stared thoughtfully at the dying match as lights began coming back on throughout the house. Joe Venuchi was going to be coming back with his goddamn hot cruiser crew pretty soon, empty-handed and sheepish. Charley Fever knew that, and he didn't need to look into any crystal balls for an answer like that.

"Well, shit," he said softly.

Then Sal Vincenti's good third arm retraced his steps across the messy porch and went down to the lawn to wipe the blood from his shoes.

This was *first* blood, he was thinking.

But a hell of a long ways, bet on that, from the *last*.

For damn sure, deadeye Bolan had been here tonight. Yeah. And the hell was just starting.

3: PENETRATED

Mack Bolan's war philosophy could be summed up in three rhyming words:

Locate . . .

Penetrate . . .

Eliminate!

Minutes into his first battle for Detroit, he was well along with that second stage of endeavor. He had been scouting this site for several days, studying it by day and by night—from land, water, and air. He had obtained building plans, landscape sketches, coastal surveys—everything that could add to his understanding of the problem. He had also studied old newspaper files, mug shots, police bulletins, and various items of quiet intelligence. He knew this enemy, and he knew their turf. He knew, also, the immensity of his task. This was no wild, amateurish adventuring into certain death. It was a carefully planned and flawlessly executed penetration of an enemy stronghold by a professional combatman. And, yes, the Executioner knew precisely where he was and what had to be done.

Except for the lakeshore side, all boundaries of the property were protected by a ten-foot rock and mortar wall. It was constantly patrolled by armed "security police" in uniform. The only landward entrance to the estate was via an interlocking system that Bolan called "the chute"—two heavily manned electronic gates positioned in a tandem arrangement fifty feet apart, with high walls and catwalks above joining the two gatehouses. A third gate was designed for exit only. It was cleverly concealed in the north wall and could be opened only by a special system of interlocks from within.

The lakeshore boundary was nearly as impenetrable, but the defenses here were almost purely human. By day and by night, armed sentries in yachting outfits prowled the boat basin and walked the seawall above the artificial beach. A secondary defense line consisting of two-man patrols walked the manicured grounds from sunset to sunrise, and there were other, less obvious, human emplacements scattered about those sprawling grounds.

There were small watchtowers on the roof of the building, as well as ominous evidence of fortifications inside.

Bolan had estimated the standing force that protected this hardsite at about eighty men, with most of that number going into the outside defenses. Except in emergency situations, the normal duty-watch consisted of twenty-five to thirty men under arms. A house crew of perhaps ten men took care of the housekeeping and doubled as inside guards. Apparently, lower echelon yardmen handled the routine chores of grounds maintenance in conjunction with the security duties. There were no "soft" employees at this joint. It was a hardsite, pure and simple.

The security boss was an old hood who went by the name of Billy Castelano—real name Reggio Caccimomorese—and whose official title was manager of the "club." Castelano had actually run a nightclub once, fronting it for a ganglord who dealt in murder by wholesale contract. A Senate subcommittee hearing in the fifties linked Castelano with more than fifty "cement contract" executions. He served a brief term in a federal reformatory for perjury and contempt of Congress, and had maintained a low underworld profile since his release.

Second in command was an ex-GI who used the name Michael Morris, nickname Mickey Mouse, real name Michael Tantocci. He'd been an MP in Germany when he was offered a "convenience of the government" discharge. This was in the early sixties, and it was a direct outgrowth of an embarrassing investigation by West German police that turned up inconclusive evidence that Tantocci was a ringleader in black market, prostitution, and extortion activities in the area. Tantocci copped a plea with the military and settled for a discharge without dishonor. He'd had no difficulty whatever adjusting to civilian life under the sponsorship of an old friend of the family, one Charles (Charley Fever) Favorini, the number one hitman of the Detroit mob. It was Charley Fever himself who had given Tantocci his mob name, Michael Morris, and further dubbed him "Mickey Mouse"—this latter due, probably, to the imaginative manner in which his fledgling assistant went about his murder contracts. At the peak of his career under Charley Fever, Mickey Morris was an acknowledged master of "freaky accidental" deaths. He was rotated to garrison duty at the yacht club when one of his "accidents" sent a lieutenant under Sal Vincenti plummeting to his undesired death in a runaway elevator that also carried four totally uninvolved passengers but none of the "transgressors" who had been marked for death.

Another crew chief at SCYC was Joseph Venuchi, a swinging ex-navy bosun's mate who now fancied himself as commodore of the yacht club—a title that he bore officially—but that, translated, actually meant he was responsible for the security of incoming shipments via water. Such shipments included contraband, narcotics, illegal aliens, bashful visiting VIPs, and the whole wide range of smuggled commodities. Venuchi's "fleet" ranged far north into Lakes Huron and Superior as well as into the easternmost reaches of Lakes Erie, Ontario, and beyond, via the St. Lawrence Seaway. He had once escorted a ranking Sicilian visitor from Montreal to Detroit and back. A casual duty of "Venuchi's navy" was to perform deep-water burials of "hot" bodies, usually in solid cement coffins.

Between Venuchi and Mickey Morris, they commanded the bulk of the hard forces that were permanently assigned to the hardsite. The success of Bolan's penetration attempt was keyed directly to his ability to neutralize a large chunk of that hard force, to send them off into a wild chase that would leave the coastal defenses in a weakened condition.

He had succeeded in this—for the moment, at least.

The problem now was to breach that weakened defense line, to penetrate the inpenetrable security of that very important mob headquarters.

It was a human problem, man against man—with all the odds riding on the defense.

But Mack Bolan was a patient warrior.

He lay suspended for an interval outside of counted time in the purgatory of Lake St. Clair, a half-submerged floater in a wetsuit at the border of hell, moving only as the waters nudged him, finally rolling into the rocks and grasses as a natural extension of the restless waves.

There he became a black rock of the night on an eroding artificial beach, while internal systems found rest, and combat senses flared into that hostile environment to assimilate the situation there.

A sentry with a suicidal need for nicotine was squatting atop the seawall about midway between the boat basin and Bolan's position—a distance of about fifty yards. He was cupping the cigarette with both hands, but sparks flew into the wind with each drag. Another guy was pacing back and forth along the pier, apparently not looking for anything but merely waiting impatiently—for the returning cruiser, perhaps.

A pair of patrolling sentries paused within ten yards of the human rock, while one of the hardmen relieved his bladder against a tree, then they continued silently upon their appointed rounds.

There were sounds up beyond the house and an occasional flare of lights at the corner of the building—vehicles in motion.

Far away and nearly buried in the silence of the night, a siren was wailing, gradually becoming louder, approaching from the south—evidently along Lake Shore Drive.

Bolan's numbers were rapidly falling together.

He made his move in a silent scramble for vegetative cover, coming to rest once again in a little hedgerow several yards beyond the waterline, where he opened the flotation bag and began rigging for close combat.

The "head weapon"—an autoloading .44 magnum—went about his waist on military web. The "quiet piece"—a Beretta Brigadier loading 9mm Parabellum hi-shockers—went beneath the left arm in a shoulder-chest rig. He called this weapon "the Belle" and had long ago equipped her with a specially engineered sound suppressor, of Bolan's own design, which muted its normally explosive report to a rustling sigh.

Utility belts bearing a miscellany of explosives and other items of survival came clipped to the rear of the automag's waistbelt. He fed these across shoulders and chest in a diagonal crossing arrangement and anchored them just above each hip, then patted each of the various items in a mental inventory that also amounted to a touch-orientation drill. In a moment of combat crisis, a soldier who intended to survive did not fumble about for his weapons—his hands found them by conditioned reflex and used them in the same frame of consciousness.

Finally he touched up the black cosmetic on hands and face and slipped on a pair of dry black sneakers. The flotation bag, empty now except for the Weatherby, went into the bushes, and the Executioner moved silently onto the hellgrounds—a flitting shadow of the night.

He made it halfway to the house before the first obstacle presented itself. A sentry with a light machine pistol suspended across his waist from a neckstrap was standing stiffly with one shoulder against a tree. He was gazing toward the lake, both hands thrust into his pockets—a melancholy figure contemplating the uncertainties of the night.

Bolan could not risk a bypass.

He moved quietly in behind the sentry and buried a nylon garrote in the soft flesh of the guy's throat, pinning the body to the tree with his own and holding it there until the frantic but totally hopeless struggle spent itself and the body sagged into dead weight. Not a sound had marred the eerie silence of that encounter. He wedged a lifeless arm into a convenient fork of the tree and left the body there, semierect and passably lifelike, except under close inspection.

A murmuring of voices cautioned him as he approached the southeast corner of the building. He went in through the flower beds and knelt there beside a budding bush in a sense-flaring recon.

There was much bustling activity at the rear. Car doors were slamming, engines idling and

28

revving, here and there voices raised in hurried farewells.

No lights were showing now from the upper level of the house, but the lower level was ablaze with light.

A large man in well-tailored threads stood in a shaft of light on a flagstoned walkway at the side, his back to Bolan. Pivoted slightly to one side in three-quarter profile was the skinny presence of Billy Castelano. The house boss was wearing white slacks and a polo shirt, no coat. A snub-nosed pistol rode in fast-break leather, shoulder-suspended over the left hip. He held a small two-way radio and was apparently relaying instructions from the big man to some remote post on the defense perimeter.

The big guy turned suddenly to gaze straight back toward Bolan. It was Charley Fever, and Bolan felt his own hackles rise. He froze and stopped breathing. The big torpedo turned away and went on with whatever he'd been telling Castelano.

Bolan abandoned that spot to move in closer to the two men.

The radio conversation had to do with the departure of a caravan of vehicles that was forming along the "quiet exit" road. As Bolan got it, they were making a big deal of what should have been a routine operation. But apparently Charley Fever had a scent of something ominous overhanging that night, and he was taking no chances with his VIP charges. He was sending them out under convoy, running fast and without lights until they were well clear of the estate. A special force was being sent beyond the north wall to protect that withdrawal and to assure the security in that sector during the time that the gate was open.

Bolan had to give the guys credit. They ran a tight operation. Somehow he had to loosen it up.

He was not after their VIP friends, not this time.

He could take them later if need be, one at a time, at his own pace.

Bolan wanted their damned hardsite. He meant to level the joint, reduce it to rubble, show them what real warfare could be, get them running scared until they were falling all over each other and bringing their own individual houses down in the panic. He wanted to see shockwaves traveling the entire length of this Detroit-based empire, which stretched around the world in every direction and into every country on the globe—an empire that controlled industries, international banks, and business cartels, multinational corporations, and even the politics of small nations. This Detroit mob was a festering sore in every vital organ of mankind. They were motivated by nothing but untempered greed and a psychotic lusting for power over other men's lives.

No, Bolan did not want their damn VIP "friends." But . . . as long as they were here, he might as well use them to whatever advantage he could.

The police sirens had become a steady wail in the night and were now very close.

It was now or never.

Bolan chose now.

He freed a hi-explosive grenade from the utility belt, armed it, and sent it lofting in a loose arc toward the roof of the joint, then immediately grabbed another and baseballed it into the vehicle area.

The transistor radio in Castelano's custody was just announcing the news from the main gate that "the cops are here. What do we . . . ?"

Fire and thunder from the roof eclipsed that report. Bloodcurdling screams came down immediately, and another voice from that sector yelled, *"Attack! Attack!"*

Castelano and Charley Fever were a pair of statues cast in frozen surprise. Another explosion, this one at ground level, unstuck their reflexes and sent them scrambling toward the front of the house.

Charley Fever gave the house boss a shove in the opposite direction and yelled at him to *"Get that caravan moving!"*

That ungentle shove sent the skinny house boss teetering practically into Mack Bolan's arms, as the other man disappeared into the shadows beside the house.

The bulbous muzzle of a black Beretta, applied directly between the brows, straightened the little man upright, and a steely arm pulled him into the darkness of the rose garden.

A quiet voice of cold precision advised the house boss, "You've got ten seconds to convince me you love life."

Castelano gasped, "God!—what!—who . . . ?"

"Close that escape gate. Five seconds to live, Billy."

Perhaps Castelano had seen too much friendly blood for one night. Certainly the memory of it

31

was etched into his awareness of the situation, and the screams from the roof could have been having their effect, also. Or perhaps he was simply a man who had become accustomed to taking orders and there was no logical alternative to the demands of the situation. Whatever his thought processes, the voice was controlled and convincing as he thumbed-on the transmitter and passed the word: "Alert countermand! Seal the walls! Nobody leaves!"

He received an excited "Ten four" from both gates, then turned a wavering smile to the big, cold guy in black. "Okay," he said calmly. "So what does that buy me?"

"A headache," Bolan replied and conked him with the butt of the Beretta. The little guy crumpled with a grunting sigh. The Executioner dropped a marksman's medal onto his chest, scooped up the radio, then moved swiftly into the tumultuous confusion of the moment.

He'd penetrated.

The rest was in the hands of the universe.

4: SOFTENED

The radio was squawking with pleas from the main gatehouse for instructions and enlightenment. The law was throwing a fit and threatening to shoot their way in—and what the hell was going on in there with all the explosions and shooting?

Alarmed sentries were apparently running in from various points on the defense perimeter. An exchange of gunfire rattled across the northwest sector. A confused enemy engaging itself?

Somewhere out there in the night a guy with a portable amplifier was ordering the hard force to get back to their stations and damn it stay there.

There was a fire on the roof. People were dashing about up there, cussing and yelling and trying to put it out with bare hands and not much else.

From the area of the north wall was issuing riotous evidence of the success of Bolan's ploy with the "quiet exit." Angered voices were raised in emotional demands and auto horns began rending the night, as the noncombatant, fleeting VIPs panicked and began reacting as they would to any frustrating traffic jam at a tense time.

A new assortment of sirens was closing in on the area from both directions along Lake Shore Drive.

The radio bleated again, this time with instructions from the yard boss: "Get those people outta those cars! Take them to the boats—to the *boats!*"

It was instant panic, the sudden softening of a very hard site, produced by a phenomenon that veteran Bolan-watchers described in cookbook terms as "a dash of Bolan."

It must have been a highly invigorating seasoning for that pot.

Barely thirty seconds had elapsed since the invader tossed that first grenade. And he was now "playing it by ear"—seizing the moment and running with the play as it developed—relying on finely tuned instincts and combat reflexes to build a victory upon the groundwork of careful planning and exhaustive intelligence that had brought the warrior to this time and place.

In Bolan's own colorful understanding, this was a matter of placing his war "in the hands of the universe." This did not mean that he was depending upon mere luck to see him through. He did not badmouth mere luck, however, and Bolan could hardly believe his good fortune when someone killed all the lights in the joint, obviously from a master panel. Everything went off at once.

The darkness was his chief ally.

At this particular moment he did not need to *see*.

They needed to see.

Apparently the enemy did not know that they had been invaded. They were still under the impression that the aggressor was *out there* somewhere.

Bolan gladly played to that misunderstanding. He whipped out a disposable-tube rocket flare, aimed the little dazzler for ignition high above the lakeshore, and let it fly. In a matter of seconds, a brilliant glow would appear in the heavens and descend slowly by parachute across the hellgrounds. It would add to the confusion, if nothing else. Meanwhile, the Executioner had business inside that joint.

He seized a heavy metal lawn chair and heaved it through a darkened ground-floor window, diving in immediately in its wake, just as the flare shell popped into brilliance high upwind.

Bolan hit the carpeted floor inside on both hands and did a handstand flip to the far wall. He lost Castelano's radio in the acrobatics but gained a precious edge in his numbers game for survival.

Two men were in that small room with him. They had apparently been seated on camp stools, close to the window, when the heavy chair came crashing through. Either they had been knocked sprawling by the chair, or their own scrambling reactions had conspired to defeat them. They were grunting and wrestling about in a tangle of limbs, camp stools, and sawed-off shotguns, trying desperately to regain equilibrium, as numbed senses thawed that frozen moment of understanding.

Bolan's equilibrium had not departed.

He came to momentary crouching rest at the opposite side of the room with silent Beretta in hand and already reflexing into the kill.

Both defenders were outlined clearly in the twilight effect from the descending flare. Each was on his knees and fighting to swing a shotgun into the firing lineup.

The Beretta chugged first and then again, two streaking pencils of flame blowing into that charged atmosphere in swift succession, a pair of 9mm shockers splattering into the twin targets with instant effect.

The guys died on their knees and toppled over into the wreckage beneath the window.

The light outside was growing by the second. The yard guy with the electronic bullhorn was beefing up the lakeshore defense line, calling hardmen by name and dispatching them to that sector.

Bolan permitted himself a brief smile of satisfaction with that, then he ventured on.

God only knew how he would get out of the joint. He would face that problem when it came up. There were more pressing problems of the moment.

He had to orient himself as to present position and mission goals. He had to make a straight-line movement across the shortest expenditure of time, energy, and space. He had to find the trembling heart of this joint and rip it out.

And, of course, he had to remain alive.

5: EXPOSED

The strong room was a super security vault. Once the locks were set from the inside, there was no way in except to convince the occupants, via an intercom, that they should let you in. It had a self-contained power and air-conditioning system, canned foods, water, other minimal comforts. A guy could sweat it out in there for a long, long time.

The last holdouts to remain in the strong room, however, were Vincenti, Tony Quaso, and the Northside boss, Pete DiLani.

"What's going on out there?" Vincenti rasped as soon as Charley Fever stepped inside.

The chief torpedo was a bit winded, and his eyes were betraying an inner excitement as he secured the door. "I think it's that Bolan guy, Sal," he reported.

"Aw, bullshit!" the *capo* yelled. "Him and what company of U.S. Marines?"

DiLani muttered, "The whole place is falling apart. I think we ought to get out of here."

"I think so, too, Pete," Charley Fever somberly agreed.

"Waitaminnit, waitaminnit there!" Crazy Sal was off again. He kicked the wall and threw a cigar the length of the room. "It's a raid, that's all —a damn police raid! It's spite, that's all! I'm going to get the guy that okayed *this* shit! I'll tack his balls to city hall and run his jock up the flagpole! These goddamn Grosse Pointe—!"

Charley Fever had moved in immediately to take his boss by the arm. "Sal, it's Mack Bolan," he said calmly, bravely interrupting the tirade. "The guy is out there with missiles or something. He's shooting flares into the yard. He's trying to level this place. He's done it to others—he might get lucky again. We need to get out of here."

"That's right," Quaso put in. "It's the way the guy operates. He don't care what he throws at you. You ought to see what I saw when I went down to Texas last week. I'm telling you—"

"Shut up, Tony!" Vincenti snapped.

"Sure, Sal. I just . . ."

"We need to move," Charley Fever urged. "Where'd the others go?"

Vincenti was glaring at a new cigar, his cheeks puffed with captured air, lips pursed angrily.

DiLani said, "They took the subway."

Charley Fever nodded his head. "That might be the best." Hawk eyes measured the emotional temperature of his boss. "Sal, that's the best."

Vincenti growled, "Awright, awright." He

smiled suddenly and said, in a softer tone, "Don't you get me killed, Charley."

The big torpedo grinned and playfully slapped his boss's shoulder. "Everybody stay close," he instructed. "We're on lights-out." He cautiously opened the door and led them out, a small pencil-flash in one hand, a Colt .45 autoloader in readiness in the other.

The noise of the night was much louder out here. Sirens were screaming all over the place. A few car horns were still blaring stupidly. Gunfire crackled here and there about the grounds—and Charley Fever had to wonder who was shooting at what. The big spotlight on the roof was on now and sweeping the area in erratic jumps from one sector to the other.

Tony Quaso mumbled, "I smell smoke."

Charley Fever explained, "Something hit the roof a minute ago."

"I thought so," Vincenti whispered in a confidential admission to his good third arm. "You really think it's Bolan?"

"I think so, Sal," Charley Fever whispered back. "Okay . . . let's go. Stay close behind me."

He led the little party across the conference room, quietly opened the door to Vincenti's private office, and quickly stepped inside. The immediate goal was a concealed door in the wall behind Sal's desk. An enclosed circular stairway went straight down to the basement, bypassing the ground floor. It was a carefully planned emergency exit, linking up in the basement with a tunnel to the lake.

The route had seldom been used for escape but had proven very handy for "quiet visits" by "friends" who, for their own reasons, did not wish to be seen by anybody save the head boss himself.

But Charley Fever's heart leapt into his mouth as he stepped into that darkened private office on this tense occasion. He was certain that he'd glimpsed the flare-out of a muffled flashlight, behind the desk.

He kicked the door shut in Sal Vincenti's face as he extinguished his own light, throwing himself sideways in the same movement, blasting away with the .45 and sending three quick rounds crashing into the wall just above desk level.

A woman's voice cried out from over there: "No! Stop that! What're you doing?"

The door banged open and Crazy Sal charged in, a revolver in each paw.

Charley Fever yelled, "Hold it, Sal! It's just a broad!"

"*What* broad?" Vincenti growled.

The good third arm had his flashlight on and was striding angrily toward Sal's desk. He lunged across and down and came up with a fistful of blonde hair, dragging a protesting young woman across the desk and spinning her to the floor at his feet. She hit with a bounce and lay there with eyes blinking groggily into the beam of light.

Tony Quaso ran in from the doorway and groaned, "Oh, good Christ! Linda!"

"You know this broad?" Vincenti raged.

"Yeah, that's my—that's Linda. You know."

"Who the hell wants to *know?*" Crazy Sal screamed. "What the hell is she *doing* here?"

"Christ, I left her in the car. She was supposed

to go back with—Linda, what the hell're you doing here? You know you ain't allowed—"

"I had to pee," the girl wailed from the floor. "And those apes ran off and left me. Yell at *them,* not a me!"

Vincenti yelled, "Hey, fuck this, *fuck* this!" He took an angry stride toward the girl then underwent one of those characteristic transformations, smiling and gallantly helping the girl to her feet. He brushed her fanny with a solicitous hand, then slapped it and told her, "There's johns all over the joint, honey. You didn't need to come way up here. I hope you didn't intend to pee in one of Papa Sal's drawers."

Charley Fever fidgeted uneasily and said, "Sal, we need to move." He shot a troubled glance toward Tony Quaso. "Bring your broad, Tony. We'll *talk* about this later." He moved behind the desk and sprung the door to the concealed stairway, then made a little gesture to the boss. "Sal?"

Vincenti was staring at a small flashlight that lay on the floor, partially under his desk. A handkerchief had been wrapped about the lens and secured there with a rubber band.

"Yeah, bring your broad," he told Tony Quaso, an eyebrow raised in another characteristic expression that meant that Crazy Sal Vincenti was thinking into a problem. "We'll take her with us. *Part* way with us, anyway."

Tony Quaso got the meaning immediately, as did the other men. The girl had been snooping at the boss's desk. And now she was to be initiated into the secret of the subway to Lake St. Clair. No way. Tony's broad was going to get *dumped* in Lake St. Clair—a long ways from shore.

The whole thing was painfully embarrassing for a second-string riser like Anthony Thomas Quaso. He growled, "I'll take care of it, Sal." He grabbed the blonde and shoved her into the lineup behind Pete DiLani. The girl went unprotestingly, contrite, head bowed. Quaso fell in behind her, and Charley Fever brought up the rear.

A faint light from below dimly illuminated the shaft. Vincenti halted about halfway down to call back, "What's that light, Charley?"

"Probably the battery lantern. The other guys must have left it on. Should be okay, Sal."

"Just the same, I don't want no more surprises. Get over to the side there, Pete. Let the guy with the broad go first."

Quaso sighed over that "the guy" putdown. He nudged the girl with his knee, and the two of them squeezed past the *capi* to head the procession.

Vincenti pulled DiLani on past, then followed by several steps. Charley Fever remained at the rear, just behind his boss.

"It's okay, Sal," he said quietly.

"Sure," Vincenti replied.

They hit the basement level and proceeded to the east side in that same order, the girl in front and guided from behind by Tony Quaso.

A lantern affixed to the far wall was throwing out a thin flood of light, the beam ending in a spot on the floor about halfway across.

Just as Charley Fever moved out of the stairwell shaft, something dark and quick blurred

42

across the lighted zone, at the head of the procession.

The blonde went hurtling off into the darkness in a plunge to the side, obviously propelled by a hard shove.

A pencil of flame leapt out to merge with the beam of the lantern and something terrible happened to Tony Quaso's head. It seemed to just burst open and fling all kinds of shit into the air.

Pete DiLani was reacting in an off-balance backward dive, digging for his pocket as he went, and he caught the same sort of problem in the throat. Charley Fever actually *saw* a flattened chunk of metal the size of a quarter erupt from DiLani's mouth, carrying with it teeth and bone and gums in a gushing spray like red vomit.

Sal Vincenti was whirling about and firing both of his pistols into the floor as he spun. He got it high in the back, near the shoulder, and this time Charley Fever heard the little whooshing sound that could only be a very effective silencer that didn't seem to be having much effect on firepower. Remembering it later (he would carry *that* memory to his grave), this professional gunman *knew* that those soft-nosed whistlers were blowing out of there under some hellish kind of muzzle velocity —very unusual for silenced weapons.

At that very moment, though, Charley Fever's mind was pitched into more urgent considerations. Without even thinking about what he was doing, he was flinging himself into a suicidal roll along that cement floor, trying to get his own bulk between those whistling missiles and the fallen body of Sal Vincenti.

He got off one shot from the Colt, firing instinctively, while realizing through some division of consciousness that he could not even see anything to shoot at. Then something like a sledgehammer hit the meaty part of his upper arm. He didn't feel a thing beyond that initial jolt, just numbness and sudden warmth. But that arm was dead from the shoulder down, and a weakness was spreading all over him. The Colt flew, and skittered across the floor.

Numbly, almost blindly, he came to his knees and got an arm under Sal. The old man was conscious, his eyes open, scared, pleading, "*Help me —help me, Charley.*"

A shadow moved up and fell across the lantern beam.

Charley Fever muttered, "It's okay, Sal."

Then he looked up, maybe even defiantly—he couldn't remember, later, exactly what his emotions were at the moment. But it was, yeah, that fuckin' guy. He was dressed in a black outfit like frogmen wear, skintight, rubbery-looking. He was dull black all over, even his face and hands, and even his damned gun was black—an automatic with the damnedest looking silencer Charley Fever had ever seen. The guy had these damned belts strung all over him and loaded down with battlefield stuff—he must have been carrying a hundred pounds of hardware. But it didn't seem to be bothering him. Tall guy, *very* tall, powerful-looking and sleek like a damned black panther, broad at the shoulders, tapering.

The worst was the goddamn eyes. They were straight from hell.

44

Charley Fever told the Executioner, in a voice so calm he surprised himself, "I'm taking Sal upstairs."

"So go," the big guy said. Like the eyes, so the voice.

Somehow Charley got the stricken *capo* onto his good shoulder and staggered away with him to the stairwell, expecting all the while to catch another sledgehammer somewhere, maybe in the head like poor Tony.

He was halfway up the stairs before he clearly realized that no more sledgehammers had come, and he could not figure that out.

Why hadn't the guy blasted him again?

Why did he do that? *So go!* Then just let him walk away like that? Why did the guy do it?

It was a question that seemed to have no answer, at least not from anywhere in the past experiences of Crazy Sal's good third arm. But it would bother him, for quite some time.

Mack Bolan himself would have been hard pressed to come up with the answer, at that moment.

Nor was he even pondering the question.

He was busy helping a blonde young lady with blazing eyes readjust her shaken dignity and professional composure.

"Damn you, Mack Bolan!" she cried, biting back the tears that were threatening to overcome what was left of her status as a liberated female. "Do you know how long I've been working on—I was this close, *this close*, to getting to the bottom of this place!"

He quietly informed her, "I was up there, Toby.

Top of the steps. I heard it. The only thing you were close to was the bottom of the lake."

"Well, damn it anyway, just *damn it!*" she fumed.

And, yeah, it *was* a very small underworld. The blonde spitfire was Toby Ranger, his swinging little buddy from the Vegas war . . . and certainly the sexiest "fed" to ever hide a badge.

6: CROSSED

Bolan had first met Toby Ranger in Las Vegas, at a moment when all his chips were riding the showdown hand. She was leader of a song and dance group called "The Ranger Girls"—and what a group. They were four of the most beautiful things on the strip, and their act was, in show biz terms, socko. It was a combination of looks and talent that could have worked all the right kinds of magic for four bright kids on their way to stardom. But these kids were working another sort of magic that Bolan did not suspect until that final, climactic moment that saw him leaving them behind, supposedly forever. The last thing Toby had said to Mack Bolan in Vegas was, "We'll cross again."

Sure. It was, after all, a small underworld. All the same, Bolan had lived many lives and died far too many deaths since that blitz through Vegas. It was a small underworld, sure, but also an infinite one for the guy who was trying to bring the whole thing down.

Friends had come and gone along that wipe-out trail. Some had simply spun off along the backwash of the man who lived on the heartbeat. One or two guys—like Leo Turrin and Hal Brognola —seemed to be unshakably tied to the Executioner's destiny. Many—too many—had been buried along that trail.

It was the latter group that weighed so heavily on Bolan's continuing forward motion. He had discovered the hard way the truth of Henrik Ibsen's declaration: "The strongest man in the world is he who stands most alone."

And he had learned that no man could stand truly alone, no matter how hard he might try. There was something in the human movement that kept tossing together people of like destiny.

So here he was, in the showdown battle of his war, with a lady fed crossing his trail once again.

No. Not even Mack Bolan could stand truly alone.

He did not, in the final analysis, live only to kill. There kept erupting those inevitable moments when something stronger than war and death entered his dimension of being. And this was one of those moments.

The battle plan was off.

All numbers were cancelled.

There might never be another clear shot at Fortress Detroit—maybe the numbers would never again fall into place—and, yes, there was agony in that decision. But it was not, in the true sense, a decision at all. It was simply a recognition of that which was.

The hit was off.

He had known it the moment he recognized the leggy blonde leading that procession to her certain death. She had abandoned her cover in Vegas to help a doomed warrior shoot his way out of an impossible situation. Now it was time to return the favor—and, no, there was no decision involved.

He dropped a marksman's medal into the gore that marked the remains of Pete DiLani, then he took the lady fed away from that hole in hell.

They found the tunnel and used it, emerging into the confusion at the boat basin just as a procession of police vehicles appeared on the circular drive near the house.

A police car with a PA system was instructing all within hearing to drop their weapons.

A boat that Bolan recognized as the cruiser that had pursued his own empty craft was moving slowly away from shore, loaded to the gunwhales with passengers.

A handful of abandoned "friends" were clustered around the two remaining hardmen in that area, and the talk was far from friendly.

Apparently the shoreline defenses had been recalled to the clubhouse, drawn there by the gunfire within.

It would be a soft withdrawal for the Executioner and his lady, with perhaps no more than one or two sentries remaining to block their path. One or two were hazard enough, of course, and the thing could yet fall apart.

Bolan told the girl, "Your buddies in blue seem

to have the situation under control. Go back if you'd like."

She shook her head. "No, that would blow everything. Lead on, Captain Puff."

He took her hand and led her southward along the lakeshore in the beginning of a journey through more hellfire than the starcrossed man from blood had ever contemplated.

The hit on the Detroit hardsite had been aborted—and the deathwatch over Detroit would find its birth in that abortion.

7: ALERTED

The Sons of Columbus Yacht Club looked like a disaster area. Police vehicles with beacons still flashing were semicircled about the clubhouse. A line of ambulances was backed into the flagstone walkway, doors open, receiving.

A fire truck stood just inside the walls, inactive. Several firemen were on the roof, tearing out smoldering shingles and tossing them to the ground.

A growing accumulation of shrouded bodies was neatly placed on the north lawn. These were beyond medical help, and were primarily a matter of statistical interest for the plainclothes cop who was moving along that lineup and peering beneath the shrouds.

He quit that inspection to halt a fast-moving litter that was headed for the ambulances. "Who shot you, Favorini?" he asked the lucky one.

Charley Fever turned a pained face toward the

detective, glared at him silently for a moment, then said, "How's Sal?"

"They're pumping blood into him," the cop replied. "He'll probably make it. Now mine. Who pumped *you?*"

"The guy didn't leave his name, Holzer," Charley Fever said, turning away with a grimace of pain.

The cop grunted to the medic and moved on. Who the hell needed names? The guy had left something even better. And a uniformed officer was at that instant hurrying over to deliver another one.

"Found this near a body in the basement, Lieutenant," the patrolman reported, handing over a military marksman's medal smeared with dried blood. "Two more DOAs down there. Tentative identification is Tony Quaso and Pete DiLani, but they're pretty messy. We'll have to rely on fingerprints for postive ID."

"Head hits," Lieutenant Holzer grunted. It was a statement of fact, not a question.

"Yes, sir. Dumdums."

Sure. The guy didn't need to leave his name.

Hell had received some wages this night, that was certain, and John Holzer had no doubts as to the identity of the collector. He dropped the little medal into an envelope, marked it, and added it to the growing collection.

The patrolman want off to find the DOA team, leaving the lieutenant to ponder the remarkable evidence of a Mack Bolan hit.

Obviously the guy was as large as his reputation. It was no secret that this Mafia "club" was better guarded than the state prison. Its defenses were regarded as second to none anywhere. Yet the guy had romped in and just laid all over them.

Nothing cute about the guy—no attempt to confuse the evidence or conceal the identity of the one responsible. Hell. He wanted them to know. Those little metal crosses were his signature—a signed confession for every crime.

And, no, it was not too difficult to piece it all together and find a coherent sequence of events.

The guy showed up first in a boat. He dropped anchor in plain view of God and everybody, and began whacking away with a high-powered rifle, dropping three of them in their tracks—head hits, in the dark, at a range exceeding several hundred yards.

Then he'd come ashore. God only knew how, with fifty rifles guarding the joint. But he did it, and apparently brought his whole damned arsenal with him. This was certified by the shaky and barely coherent story of Billy Castelano, perhaps the luckiest man of the night, and didn't he know it. Castaleno had sat in the grass, clutching a marksman's medal in his hand and groaning. While a medic worked on a bleeding skull laceration, Castelano babbled about grenades and "combat stuff" and how the guy suddenly appeared "right out of thin air."

Holzer knew that Mack Bolan did not possess supernatural powers. But there *was* something uncanny about the guy. They had found the dead sentry propped into the fork of a tree, then Holzer had worked a hunch and straight-lined the guy, tracing him back to the most probable point of landing. A few minutes later the bushbearers discovered the rubber bag containing nothing but a sheaf of ballistics charts, trajectory graphs, and optic calibrations for a Weatherby .460—which bore out Holzer's earlier diagnosis of a hi-punch weapon figuring into the first three casualties.

Supernatural, no. Supermilitary, yeah.

The weapon was obviously equipped with the most sophisticated optic system Holzer could imagine, and the papers left behind indicated that even this basic accessory had been further refined by a guy who knew what he was about.

The weapon belonged to a guy who worked for what he got. It wasn't as easy as he made it look.

And, sure, John Holzer could respect this man, this determined fugitive who had violated just about every law in the book.

Nothing in the book of rules said you had to *hate* the guy. In the still quiet recesses of his unofficial mind, Holzer even *envied* the guy. How nice it would be to cut through the maze of red tape and official legalities . . . to just pick up a weapon and go *hunting* for these cruds.

Yeah. But he couldn't do that.

He trudged back to his vehicle, got in, sighed, and reached for communications.

"This is Hotel One," he told the dispatcher. "Code this for Metropolitan Alert and clear me through to Detroit Central. Also a conference patch to the federal task force, Artillery Armory."

"Stand by, Hotel One," came the instant response.

While Holzer "stood by," his gaze swung magnetically along the still growing row of sheet-draped litters across that lawn.

"Stand by, hell," he muttered into the night.

Then his connection came through, and he commenced the broadcast that had become a part of the contingency plans of every law enforcement agency in the area, including federal and Canadian.

The alert was on.

The hunter had become the hunted.

And, for this one, there was nothing to be envied. There would be no red tape and no official legalities. The plan was clear. Mack Bolan was to be shot on sight.

8: REALIZED

Toby hated to admit it even to herself, but she definitely felt better with the big fellow around. He was a nice solid rock to lean upon, and it just didn't make any sense to fight him. Toby needed a rock to lean on at the moment . . . and it felt good just to acknowledge that fact.

She watched from the background as he silently and methodically disposed of the guard at the southern boundary, then she trotted beside him for what seemed a mile. It was too much effort to attempt conversation, and there was not that much to be said. He slid her a reassuring glance from time to time and paused twice to wait for her while she made necessary adjustments to the ridiculous shoes she was wearing.

She was beginning to wonder if he intended to lope all the way to town, when he suddenly took a ninety-degree swerve and led her inland through the darkened grounds of a large estate. The place appeared deserted. He had stashed a car in there, close to Lake Shore Drive—and she had an opportunity to again watch the man at work, in the grimmest business of all—survival.

He pressed her to the ground beside a prickly shrub, within sight of the car, quietly commanded her to "stay put," and then he simply vanished. One moment she was watching his circular advance toward a stand of trees lining the driveway; the next moment he just wasn't there. It was not all that dark a night. She began to fidget with uneasiness as time lengthened and no perceptions of the man crossed her senses. Then she caught a glimpse of a fleeting movement out near the roadway, and she understood what he was doing.

In the military, they would call it reconnoitering.

Mack Bolan probably called it surviving.

Very grim, yes, this man's business.

He reappeared beside her a couple of minutes after that, showing her a reassuring flash of eyes and teeth, and she went with him to the stashed vehicle.

He held the door for her, then went to the rear and opened the luggage compartment.

She heard heavy items being deposited back there and suddenly realized that the big quiet man had carried a lot of extra weight along that mile's worth of run. Toby herself was just beginning to breathe normally. She weighed a hundred and ten pounds and enjoyed the superb conditioning of a professional dancer. What fantastic sort of conditioning did this man enjoy?

A glimpse of bare torso reflected in the car mirror went a long way toward answering that question; telling her, also, that he was changing clothes. She quickly angled the mirror for a few adjustments to her own appearance, which was somewhat the worse for this night's work, and tried to forget that stolen glimpse of Captain Beautiful. It was a damn silly time to get a rush over a male body, especially that one.

Don't be dopey, Toby, she scolded herself. You're on opposite sides of the fence. Mack Bolan is a hunted fugitive. A tragic, *tragic* man. Emergency coexistence for mutual survival is one thing, it's forgivable. But don't entertain dreamy ideas about Captain Hormone back there. That man is riding a one-way ticket to hell. *That* man . . .

He slid in beside her, destroying that mental lecture. He now wore slacks and a dark shirt, open at the neck. Draped about the shoulders was a towel that he was using to remove that black makeup.

She told him, "I'll do that. Let's go."

He tossed the towel to her and started the car moving, easing onto Lake Shore Drive and turning smoothly southward. She came to her knees on the seat and leaned against him as she dabbed the cosmetic away from that granite face.

"Well . . . it's been a lovely evening," she said. "Where now, Captain Marvelous? Your place or mine?"

He slid his gaze toward her and replied, "I can drop you wherever you'd like."

Toby let the matter hang while she vigorously scrubbed his forehead. It was necessary, of course, to get him in a headlock to hold that stubborn head

58

steady under the assault. And she could not resist planting moist lips in the heart of the clean spot. Then she did his face and hung a couple of swift ones there, also.

"Call it thanks," she murmured. "I *was* in a bad spot. Thanks."

"Forget it," he growled.

She flung the towel at him and said, "Okay, so I spoiled your timing or something tonight. But I didn't ask you for a damn thing. Why are you always so surly with me, Mack Bolan?"

He showed her an obviously forced smile, and the voice was softer as he replied, "Sorry. Nothing personal, Toby."

Sure. She understood. Nothing personal. All business, grim, unyielding. Boy, she'd had a hope chest full of *that!* She experienced a sudden desire to just start screaming and bawling all at once.

She flounced to the far corner. murmuring, "What a lousy life you lead, Mack Bolan."

"*We* lead," he reminded her.

Hell, that was all it took. She let it out, then, not as the screaming fit she desired but as silent tears blinding and humiliating her, followed swiftly by detestably weak damn feminine gulps and gobbles as she fought to shut it off and tuck it all back in.

Bolan reached for her, and she slapped his hand away. He grabbed her anyway and jerked her over against him, then held her there in an enfolding arm, her head on his chest.

She cried, "Damn you, Bolan!" then melted into the embrace, allowing herself to be comforted as every woman has a right to be from time to time.

59

"It's okay," he told her in an incredibly soft voice.

"The hell it is," she blubbered. "I'm a cop, damn you. How many cops have you ever done this for?"

"Men cry, Toby," he said, and there was nothing impersonal, grim, or unyielding in that quiet declaration. It was a confession, a statement of equality, not condescending comfort.

She saw the man then, the *true* man, in a blinding flash of understanding. And the tragedy of his life deepened in that understanding. It had to do with *personal* versus *impersonal* and a paradox in those terms. A man with genuine human warmth and depth cloaked himself in cold purpose and grim necessity, then went out to kill and destroy in a purely impersonal crusade, yet somehow managing to retain that deeply personal dimension of self that could and probably did often revolt against the grim game.

But the man on the stage of death was the impersonal one.

In contrast, a brutal, mad dog of a man, totally lacking in human qualities, could masquerade as a genuine human being to spread misery wherever his strongly personal desires focused, and without once experiencing a revolt of personality.

Men cry, Toby.

Yes, sure they did. *Real* men.

Mack Bolan was real, this was Toby's illumination. Her tears ceased almost immediately, and she snuggled into the reality of the man, accepting him, accepting herself, saving the revolt for those who deserved it.

They drove silently on, the journey ending a

few minutes later in a modern apartment complex somewhere on the north side. He put the car in an underground garage, and they shared a silent elevator to the twelfth floor of the highrise, then he led her to a nicely appointed efficiency apartment that overlooked the city.

"Who'd you have to hit to get this?" she asked him.

"Sublet, one week," he told her. "No questions asked, just lots of money."

She inspected the place with a personal interest, looking for further clues to the man, realizing almost at once that she would find none. The warrior lived here, not the man.

Next-to-invisible threads on doors and windows revealed his preoccupation with security against undetected callers.

He traveled light.

A single change of clothing was all the closet held. The bathroom boasted toothbrush and toothpaste, razor, comb, bar of soap, and towel.

He had gone directly to the studio kitchen and was making coffee.

She watched him for a moment, then asked, "Are you inviting me to stay? Or did I miss something?"

Without looking up from his task, he told her, "I'm suggesting that you do."

"Why?"

He said, "I goofed. Allowed Charley Fever to walk away with a light hit. He'll be wondering about you. And me. Might put something together." He looked up then, fixing her with a sober gaze. "That is, unless you'd rather chuck your cover and put on your badge. Even then, he could decide to put you on contract. These guys are edgy."

She bit her lip and thought about that.

"I'll stay," she decided. "Flip you for the first shower."

"I was hoping we could have a cooperative venture," he said, showing her the first genuine smile of the night.

She edged a hip against a wall and folded her arms across her chest, very soberly. Her eyes studied the floor as she replied, "Just what did you have in mind?"

"Forget it. I thought we were both pros, that's all."

"Yes?"

He turned back to the coffee and said, "Sorry. Forget it."

"Captain Bluff," she said, half angrily.

"Go to hell," he said.

"If you're going to start it, you should finish it."

"You're the cop. You finish it."

She tossed her head and moved away from the wall, arms remaining folded over the chest. "What kind of pros are we?"

Bolan lit a cigarette and blew smoke toward the coffeepot. "I said, forget it."

She could not. "If that was a cheap shot, Mack, I'm terribly disappointed in you."

"No shot at all," he muttered.

"Okay. I'm a pro. A whore with a badge. Is that what you meant? I've been playing bedsy with Tony the Louse Quaso for the past month. If you expect me to apologize for that, forget it, just *you* forget it."

He told her quietly, "Toby, I've killed more men this week than you've screwed in a lifetime. And I don't *have* a badge. I'm not throwing stones your way."

She said, miserably, "Damn it. Just damn it."

He watched her through a moment of silence, then dropped his cigarette in the sink and ran water on it. "Look," he said, finally, "I felt a sudden desire to scrub your back. Okay? Person to person, man to woman, and to hell with everything else for a little while. What I said about professionals had nothing to do with whoring and killing. I simply meant that people like you and me lead a special sort of existence. There's no time or opportunity for all the cute romancing, for waltzing around the floor 'til dawn, gazing deeply into each other's eyes. We live on an entirely different level. We have to *love* on that level, or not at all. That's what I meant, and that's all I meant."

"Did you say *love?*"

"Yeah," he growled. "Remember what that is?"

"I do," she replied solemnly. "Do you love me?"

"Tonight, Toby, I could love Dracula's mother. No, uh, comparison intended."

She giggled. "Okay, Captain Pro. Flip you for the first back scrub."

"You're on," he said.

And then she was being lifted off her feet, clasped in strong arms, carried to the doorway of a very special reality.

Emergency coexistence, that was it . . . for

63

mutual survival. And personal . . . wow, *was* it personal!

Captain Virile could and would wash away the revolting stage stains of Tony the Louse.

Mack Bolan was for real.

9: DIVERTED

He awoke with the dawn, knowing that it could be his last, aware and thankful that he was here for this one.

The woman beside him was now a very special leaf in his growing book of life. He had known her in various guises, liked and respected her in each. Now he knew her in her essences, having gained that knowledge in the only way possible.

Do you love me?

Of course, he loved her. He'd loved all of them, each of them being unique in her own special way, yet all of them one and the same in that larger identity: essential woman. The story of Adam and Eve could be pure fable, but the guy who thought it up must have lived the story first.

It is not good that the man should be alone.

I will make him a helpmeet for him.

"Helpmeet." That meant partner. Sure, the guy had known what it was to be alone. And he'd known, surely, that very special quality of *woman* that truly was a *helpmeet* for all those challenged devils on whom had been placed the onus of life and survival on a hostile planet.

Bolan knew—survival meant more than a quick gun and fast reflexes. Every man alive faced the same challenge that was Bolan's—faced it according to the dictates and the needs of each of life's situations.

Life was no accident, hell. Much bigger than that, life was some sort of special cosmic magic that gave meaning to that infinity of non-life filling the blackness of space.

Doctor, lawyer, Indian chief . . .

Sure, all of them, each of them, every man had his challenge, his own unique road to survival, his own special . . . what? Special *what?*

Cosmic magic, maybe. What were we surviving? Every man died sooner or later. So . . . surviving what?

Surviving the *onus,* maybe—those special conditions that fell into a man's bag of life to bedevil him, goad him, stir him up, move him out onto the road to somewhere.

That was it. The guy had to survive the *challenge.* Which simply meant that he had to *meet* it. Yeah, with every damn thing he had. No ducking allowed, no dodging. Head on, eye to eye and toe toe, fight like hell and end up there if that's what it takes—but *beat the damn challenge.*

And, yeah, for that, a man needed a partner.

But Bolan had learned that women had need of "helpmeets" also. Not just the Toby Rangers, but all of the desperately challenged creatures everywhere. Women had special challenges.

A man needs a woman, and a woman needs her man.

Sure. Guys wrote songs about it. Other guys had written entire psychiatric journals on the subject. What it all boiled down to was *person* to *person*—and beyond, *man* to *woman.*

No man could stand truly alone. Once in a while there had to be another human being to whom he could turn, and with whom hopefully he could merge for a while, to recharge the belief that survival was worthwhile, to see beyond himself into that cosmic sprawl of uncommon magic. Nowhere else had Bolan observed the magic of the cosmos in such clear and striking reference as in the eyes of a good woman in honest passion. All of it was there, all of the magic, and Bolan knew that it was good. In that glimpse he knew that life was worthwhile, that the challenge was necessary, and that *survival* was the whole goal.

A message, maybe, *through a helpmeet,* from the guy who started it all?

Well, maybe. All Bolan knew for sure was that he felt better for the experience. And it wasn't just that moment of bliss that made human sex such an ennobling exercise. It went a hell of a lot deeper than that.

He pulled his woman over atop him and playfully slapped that delightful highrise bottom. "Hey, cop," he growled.

"How profane," she groaned. "And after all we've been through together."

"Time to rise and shine."

She giggled sleepily. "That's your department."

He slapped her again, more briskly.

She yowled and rolled away, coming to rest slumped upon the edge of the bed, feet on the floor "Give me a push," she requested in a small voice. "Maybe I can make it."

"Make it where?"

"To the bathroom, Captain Ignorant. Don't you know anything about girls? We puke every morning after. That's a reaction to male exploitation."

Bolan chuckled.

She declared, small-voiced, "If I try very hard, I'll bet I can make it. But then I'll probably never walk again."

He told her, "Nothing visibly wrong from here. You look all systems go."

"Went, Captain Ecstasy. *Went.*"

He pushed her with his foot. She slid to the floor and sat there, cross-legged, scowling back at him.

He said, "If it's all that bad, hell . . . give it back."

She turned away, head drooping toward the floor. Mack . . . ?"

"Yeah."

"Thanks."

"You're welcome."

"I mean, pardon the cliché, I needed that."

He told her, "We both did."

"So what now?" she asked, still drooping. "Will you marry me?"

"Marry a cop? Me?"

She laughed quietly. "That would be far out, wouldn't it? Well . . . I guess I've got to marry somebody."

"Yeah?"

"Yeah. For the first time in my life, I feel like an ex-virgin."

"Is it that bad?"

"It's that *good*," she said.

"Well . . . Toby . . . Maybe we'll cross again . . . somewhere."

"Let's quit. Both of us quit. The business, I mean."

"What would that solve?"

She swiveled that lovely head about to gaze at him over a rose petal shoulder. "For you, I guess, nothing."

"And for you?"

She shrugged daintily. "I don't know. I get confused, Mack. I don't know what the hell it's all about, even. You ever get that way?"

He told her, "Yeah. Occupational hazard. But it passes."

She sighed. "Mack . . ."

"Yeah?"

"I'm not on an assignment. Not officially."

"What are you on, then?"

"I'm looking for Georgette."

"For who?"

"You remember Georgette Chableu. The Canadian—"

Sure he remembered. The body shop, tall, dark, and juicy, the Canuck member of the Ranger Girls. "What's happened to her?"

"That's what I've been hoping to find out. Logic tells me that she's dead. But I have to *know*. You understand?"

Bolan understood. People who lived large also

69

grieved large, and there was no shrugging off the uncertain fate of a comrade in arms.

He left the bed and pulled the girl to her feet, then hustled her along to the bathroom, where they shared another shower, much briefer and considerably more subdued this time. Later he shaved while she put a breakfast together, and it was not until they were facing each other across the dining table that the conversation was resumed.

"Tell me about it," Bolan commanded.

She nibbled daintily at crisp bacon and said, "Well . . . where do I start? Some background, I guess. Toronto, let's start there. It's Georgette's home town. They've been having this problem for —oh, I guess a couple of years. Small at first, but growing all the time. Now the Canadian authorities are in full alarm. Girls disappearing, see. I mean, vanishing. Never to be seen again. Each of the victims is a kid, still in her teens or barely out of them. All beautiful. All from the edge of show business and—"

"Which edge?"

Toby wrinkled her nose. "Mostly legitimate. A few of the victims had been playing around with porno movie makers. But most were just kids looking for a legitimate start somewhere. Beauty contestants, singers, go-go girls, you know the routine. Someplace to showcase beauty, a speck or two of talent, and a dream. A lot of those dreams turned to nightmares, I'd guess."

Bolan sipped his coffee, then stared into the cup with see-nothing eyes. "Prostitution, eh?"

"That's the general impression. But not *just* prostitution."

"Slavery." He spat it, like a bad taste in his mouth.

"That's the nice name. Two of the victims turned up recently. One was found in the gutter of a Mexican border town, across the Rio Grande from Texas. She was dead from a heroin overdose. The other took the quick way down from the top of a posh resort hotel near Acapulco."

"Canada to Mexico," Bolan muttered.

"For those two, yes."

"Sending prostitutes to Mexico," he commented heavily, "is like carrying coals to Newcastle."

"Toronto thinks that Mexico is just one stop on an international circuit. Big time. Jet set party girls, sort of. This idea is based mostly on the missing girls themselves. They're not just pretty girls, Mack. They're spectacular girls, without exception."

"Will it never end?" Bolan growled.

"Name of the game, friend," Toby replied soberly. "Sex for sale is damned big business, or hadn't you heard?"

"For sale or *trade*," he reminded her. "Some guys will sell their souls to hell for a free peek into that cosmic sprawl."

"What?"

"Pet theory of mine regarding the basis of sex. Forget it. What about Georgette now?"

"Well, back to Toronto. They decided that the victims were either kidnapped or lured with false promises. Which means, then, that most of the girls will have to be broken. You know the routine."

Yes, Bolan knew the routine. Terror, repeated rape, degradation, shame, drugs—and, if nothing else worked, the threat of "dirty pictures" being sent home to families and friends.

Toby was continuing the report. "Georgette has this friend in Toronto who is someone big with the police establishment. I don't know the whole story, but I do know that the contact was made through our office in Washington. She got a release from Washington and volunteered to help Toronto with the usual undercover gig. Georgie's a real phantom at that stuff, as you should know."

Yes, Bolan knew. "This was when?"

"About six weeks ago. She took a job at one of the suspect places, go-go girl. Had one meeting with her contact man a few days after she started. She reported at that time that she had been introduced to Tony Quaso, but not by that name. He was posing as a talent agent from New York, but she recognized him immediately. As the story went, he was supposed to return the next night with another agent, to catch her routine. Toronto had her under constant surveillance. They had her room bugged, two of their men had jobs in that club. But Georgette vanished a few hours after that report to her contact. Hasn't been seen or heard from since."

"Six weeks," Bolan growled.

Toby tossed her head and said, "I gave her a couple of weeks to surface. Then I asked the home office to put me on the case. They didn't say no. They said hell no. So . . . I hadn't had a real vacation for two years. I had leave coming and I took it."

Bolan sighed. Half of his breakfast remained untouched and forgotten. He lit a cigarette and glared at the wall. Finally he said, "So you cultivated Tony Quaso."

She nodded her head and made a wry face. "I figured that would be the most direct approach."

"So what did you learn?"

"Not much, I guess. But I was getting there, until tonight. And I did get at least a sniff of Georgette's trail. I believe they found out about her federal connection."

"What made you think that?"

"Personal experience I had. I walked into Quaso's joint out here on Six Mile Road and asked for a job. The manager auditioned me and hired me on the spot. I was billed as Linda Lakemont but I was on the payroll as Linda Walters. Three nights after I started, Quaso himself came in during the last act and issued a royal summons for me to join him at his table. One of the bartenders brought the drinks, in a joint that has a cocktail waitress for every three tables. That put my teeth on edge, and I was scared to death to drink it, but I did. Then the same bartender came back for the empties. He used the old two finger trick when he picked up my glass. You know, two pinkies inside to preserve the fingerprints outside."

"You think they ran a make on you?"

"I know they did. Soon as I got away from there I beat it to a Washington hotline and passed the word to my buddy in the fingerprint bureau. He punched my prints into the computer as Linda

73

Williams, with a bust in Houston for indecent exposure and lewd performance in a public place. The very next day I got the tip from Washington that an official ID request had come in through regular police channels. It's no secret that the mob owns cops everywhere. Well, later when Quaso and I became pals, he just had to get cute and let me know that he knew about my sordid past. I pouted then, until he told me how he found out. He said they'd had some trouble a while back with 'a broad' who'd been playing games with them. Since then, they were taking pains to know who they were playing with."

"He made no bones about his underworld connections?"

"He bragged about it," Toby said. "Shall I tell you how many times I had to sit through *The Godfather?*"

"He's not bragging now," Bolan said quietly. "So I loused up your direct connection. I'm sorry."

"Don't be," she said. "I already had all I was going to get from Tony the Louse. I think that place out there on Grosse Pointe is holding some secrets, though."

"Is that just instinct? Or do you have something solid?"

"About half and half. One night after Quaso and I had . . . gone to bed, he got a call from someone in Toronto. It was just monosyllables from our end, but I caught a word or two from Toronto. Something about a special shipment of meat, great stuff, that kind of talk. Quaso wrote something on a pad by the phone. Next morning the pad was clean, but I picked the impressions off the sheet below. It was just two groups of numerals. One was 1492—fourteen ninety-two—the other was a time, 6:30. Now what does 1492 suggest to you?"

Bolan muttered, "Columbus sailed the ocean blue."

"Right. And the Sons of Columbus have themselves a dandy little yacht club smack on the Canadian border."

"Okay, it could mean something."

"Sure, it could."

He sighed. "You need help, Toby."

"Is that an offer?"

"Helpmeet."

"What?"

He showed her a sober smile. "The Canuck helped save my skin once."

"I guess it's an offer," she said, giving him a perplexed gaze. "I, uh, I couldn't have asked you, Mack. You've got enough to . . ."

He said, "I need a new angle of attack, anyway."

"Well . . ."

"We need to hit directly at the source."

"Toronto?"

He nodded glumly. "You still have a pilot's license?"

"Sure. I'm Toby. Fly me anywhere."

"You'll have to leave your badge at home."

"Oh, sure. I told you, I'm on leave."

"I'm the boss. You do what I say when I say it."

"You're the boss," she agreed soberly. "When do we start?"

"How does five minutes sound?"

She leaned across the table to plant a kiss on his lips, holding her own there in light contact as she told him, "Like music, Captain Quick. Like a fresh new sound from a fresh new place. God loves you, Captain Wonderful."

Bolan wasn't so sure about God, but the message from the helpmeet was very clear.

And, this time, he couldn't decide whether it was good or bad.

Necessary, though, yeah. Cosmic magic, maybe.

The *onus*, for damned sure.

10: BACKTRACKED

Toby first placed a brief call to Toronto—then she rented a Beechcraft single-engine job, and they flew due north out of Detroit before angling eastward across Lake Huron for the penetration of Canadian airspace.

She was a good pilot and an excellent seat-of-the-pants navigator. They crossed the width of the Ontario boot and reached Toronto without incident, putting down at a small field near the shoreline of Lake Ontario.

A few brief words from Toby cleared a path there and saw them speeding into the city, minutes later, in a rented car.

Bolan did not ask, nor was he told about the "special arrangement" that the girl enjoyed. He suspected that it had to do with Georgette's "someone big with the police establishment." He knew that someone with considerable authority, and probably great concern for the fate of the missing

77

policewoman, was working some magic for them.

They reached the "suspect place" on Toronto Harbour while the day was still young. Following Bolan's instructions, Toby canvassed the neighborhood in two slow passes, then she parked directly at the entrance to Simon's Grotto, a "girls girls girls" joint that apparently catered to the waterfront crowd.

The girl remained with the vehicle while Bolan made a frontal assault on the problem. He wore a dark, neatly tailored suit, nylon turtleneck, and the Beretta Belle.

Simon's was dark, reeking with a thousand identifiable odors, and mostly empty of patrons. A narrow doorway with a chair placed in the opening divided the joint—into day and night, probably.

"Day" was a long bar with greasy wooden stools and a line of small tables along the outside wall.

"Night" was a fair-sized lounge with many tables jammed close together, now with chairs upended atop them. A large stage spanned the far end.

There was a smaller stage in the day room, behind the bar. It held a couple of wicker props and a life-sized poster of a fetching filly called Tootles LaFleur, below which was scrawled the announcement: Luncheon Show.

Yeah. Bolan could see it with his inner eye: luncheon with Tootles—bare bouncing boobs with beer and a cheese sandwich and pretzels to lift a guy briefly from deadening monotony and hopeless mortality. Sure, every man sought his own cosmic magic at the level available.

The guy behind the bar had no magic left whatever. He gave Bolan a disinterested greeting and waddled along the backbar like a walrus on his final march to the sea.

"No lunch 'til eleven," the barman announced from several paces back. "You want beer, we got—"

"Where's the boss?" Bolan growled.

"What?"

He pinned the guy to his tracks with a fierce glare and a voice of sheer ice. "The man, damn it!"

"Oh, he uh . . ."

"Don't screw around. It's a long way from Detroit."

"Oh, sure," the walrus said, glad to be relieved of further thought and, therefore, responsibility. "Just through the door there, turn left. Office is behind the stage. You'll find it."

Bolan found it with no difficulty whatever and with no loss of time. He was moving quickly along a narrow hallway when the door presented itself, bearing the neat sign: "Mister Simon. Private."

Bolan presented the door with two hundred pounds moving fast behind a driving foot, and the flimsy thing splintered away in full surrender.

Two guys were seated at a table along the back wall. One was stacking currency, the other was feeding coins into a counting machine—or, that's what they had been doing.

Now they were lunging onto their feet and grabbing for revolvers that were perhaps no more than a heartbeat too far away. The Belle leapt into that void and sealed it there—one heartbeat away —with a pair of rustling little persuaders that had no respect whatever for the privacy of mere flesh and bone.

One of the guys spun into the wall. The other hit the corner of the table and the whole thing went over.

A fortyish guy behind a rickety desk gasped, "My God! My *God!*"

The guy had no god, and he must have known it right away. Both hands immediately shot skyward, and he stammered, "No—not armed—wait!"

Bolan went over there and placed the warm muzzle of the Belle at the center of Mister Simon's forehead.

"Take it!" the guy gasped. "Hell, it's yours, I'm giving it to you. Take it!"

The icy Bolan gaze slid disdainfully to the scattered stacks of bloodsoaked currency. "That? I didn't come for that."

He kept the Beretta where she belonged and flipped a marksman's medal onto the desk. "Pick it up," he commanded.

Simon picked it up, then dropped it with a shivery jerk. "Oh, my God! Hey, I'm not—*no!* Wrong guy! My God, I'm not Mafia!"

Bolan told him, "You stink like it, guy."

"I'm not! I swear! Let me prove it! I'll cooperate! Tell me what you want. Hey, just tell me!"

"Girls girls girls," Bolan intoned coldly. "At wholesale prices. What's the going price of *one* girl, Simon? About fourteen ninety-two?"

"What? *What?* Hey, hey, look now! I'm a supplier, that's all. After that I don't know nothing! I swear!"

The Belle pressed her advantage, and the guy's head went to full backward tilt. Now he was staring straight up toward his forlorn god. "You better think up something better than that, guy," the voice from hell advised him.

"Well, God, give me a hint! What d'you want?"

"Your goof, Simon. Not theirs. Now it's too late. I don't deal for dead girls, guy."

"Well, wait! Wait now! Which girl was it?"

Bolan produced a glossy photo of Georgette and held it above the guy's bulging eyes. Simon wilted a bit more as he breathed, *"That* one."

"That one."

"Well, I don't think she's *dead*," the guy said, choking around the acute curve of his distorted throatline. "Lets talk—hey, look. Let's discuss this like reasonable men. I want to help you. I can't help you if I'm dead."

Bolan seemed to consider that for a second, then he eased off and told Simon, "You've bought ten seconds' worth of reasonableness."

"What can I do in ten seconds?"

"Five, now."

The guy's eyes rolled in their sockets, and he screamed, *"They found out about her!"*

"Found out what?"

"She's a cop! What the hell, I had nothing to do with that! I just supply them."

"Too bad," the iceman replied, and the Belle bore back in.

The guy screamed, loud and frantically, *"She's not dead!"* Spittle was trickling down his chin, and a vein in his neck was pulsing much too rapidly.

Bolan eased off again, as much for his own sake as anything else. The guy could die without any help at all at this point, and that was not the name of Bolan's game.

He told Simon, "Okay, you bought another ten seconds."

"God, Jesus—thanks, thanks. I'm leveling with you, Mr. Bolan. I want to help you."

Bolan was not, of course, overly certain of that. A dying man would say most anything, if he feared death enough. He stepped back a pace and sheathed the Beretta. The guy was in a half faint, wobbling in his chair, eyes swinging dully from side to side. The head found its natural level, and the guy stole a quick glance at the men on the floor. Horrified eyes jerked back quickly, skittered away from Bolan, came to rest on his own hands, which were now splayed out across the top of the desk, knuckles white with desperation.

"I want the girl, Simon," Bolan said calmly. "And you've got *no* seconds, guy, none at all left now."

In a voice hoarsened from violent emotion, Simon said to the Executioner: "I'll show you all I have to show. I have to get on my feet. And I'll show you."

Bolan pulled the guy out of the chair and steadied him against the side of the desk. There was no compassion for this man, this dealer in human degradation. He would squash a thousand guys like this one without a tremor if that would save one girl one hour of the fate dealt to them by these cannibals.

All of that loathing and disgust was hanging

there in plain view as Bolan told the soul merchant, "So show me."

Toby was fidgeting and peering anxiously at the entrance to Simon's Grotto when Bolan emerged from a doorway farther along the wharf and returned briskly to the car.

He slid in beside her and said, "Let's go."

She put the car in motion as she asked him, "How'd you get way down there?"

"These guys love tunnels," was all he said.

They cleared the neighborhood and were circling toward the throughway before the girl prodded him with a quiet, "Well?"

"I got what I came for," he told her. "Let's get back to the plane." He saw the agitation in her eyes and added, "Hang onto hope, Toby. Our gal could still be alive. Call your friend from the airport. Tell him he's been watching the wrong point. They move the stuff through Simon's floor and along an old storm drain. Drop it into small boats that can get under the wharf. The drop point is about two-hundred yards west of Simon's. They move the girls the same way. Rendezvous with a larger craft out beyond the harbor. Incoming stuff takes the same route in reverse."

She nodded impatiently. "I'll pass the word. But what about Georgette?"

"That's the part you don't pass along," he replied. "Not until I say different. Timing is all important now. I don't want any police movements upsetting that."

"Georgette, damn it."

"You're going to have to trust me, Toby. More than I trust you. When—"

"That's a hell of a thing to say!" she protested.

"Maybe so," Bolan growled. "But that's the way it has to be. You can hope, but not too loudly. Beyond that, you just have to trust that I'm doing what needs doing, and go along quietly."

She fumed, "Well that's the damnedest, most outrageous . . ."

It was a bad shot, sure, but a relative cruelty. Toby had too much of her own ass into the problem. If Bolan told her everything he'd learned and begun to suspect about the current status and possible fate of Georgette Chableu, then he chances were pretty good that Toby would lose professional cool and charge off in a disastrous direction. She did not need that extra burden, and Bolan did not intend to impose it upon her, regardless of what she might be thinking at the moment.

"Trust me," he said quietly.

Her hands whitened on the steering wheel, and that determined little jaw took on a harsher set, but she told him, "Okay, Captain Granite. But you'd better be as good as I think you are."

He hoped he was.

They drove through several minutes of silence, then Toby asked him, "Did you leave anyone alive back there?"

"Are you," he replied coldly, "kidding?"

He began hauling packets of red-stained currency from his coat pockets as he gruffly reported, "I made it look like a heist. And there's no one to tell any other tale."

"Captain Perfect," she breathed, through clenched teeth.

Yeah.

Bolan hoped so.

He was returning to Detroit to resume the deathwatch. That new "angle of attack" had presented itself. And it was no coincidence whatever that Georgette Chableu, dead or alive, lay directly across that path.

11: BAITED

The police conference at Detroit Central had been brief and to the point. An inspector out of the DPD chief's office was designated as "skipper" —or, chief administrative officer—of the joint police effort. This was Jason Garvey, a shrewd and capable man who had once held an associate professor's chair in police administration.

An organized crime specialist from the attorney general's office in Lansing was named as executive officer. Representatives from every police district and jurisdiction in the area fleshed out the "strategy board"—a sort of planning commission for the unified strike force.

A "contingencies unit" was formed under Lieutenant John Holzer of Grosse Pointe. Federal and Canadian representatives were present in advisory-liaison capacities. Two "observers" from the state house also attended the conference.

Special communications nets were established and "regional reaction" plans set into motion.

The deputy superintendent for DPD dropped in for a quick off-the-cuff pep talk—reminding those present of the "tense law enforcement situation" in the tricounty area and sounding a sober warning of the possible consequences of a Mack Bolan invasion into that situation.

A special federal liaison officer briefed the conference on the "life and war" of Mack Bolan, with particular emphasis on general *modus operandi* and "profile goals."

The fed said, "Contrary to much rumor and speculation, the federal government has given no secret sanction to this illegal crusade. The U.S. Department of Justice regards Mack Bolan in the same light as any other fugitive from justice. Law enforcement officers must not stake their lives on the romantic notion that this highly dangerous fugitive has never shot it out with the law and therefore never will. In fact, a recent profile by a convention of noted medical psychologists indicates that this subject has already progressed well beyond the breaking point of sound physical endurance—that he is probably in an advanced state of psychosis and should be regarded as totally out of control. In other words, he is capable of committing any act. A man of such awesome destructive capabilities must not and cannot be allowed the freedom of your streets."

The speech by the fed was recognized by many lawmen present as a plea for rank-and-file professionalism in the campaign to get Bolan. It was no great secret that many police officers sympathized with the man's crusade and would, in fact, turn their backs if they encountered Mack Bolan on the street.

John Holzer had his own private opinion of the federal "briefing."

"Bullshit," he said disgustedly to a man at his table. "Bolan is the sanest man in town right now. Deadly, yeah—insane, hell no. I wish I had a dozen cops with half that much sanity. Maybe I'd catch the dude."

The general plan that unfolded through the police conference involved close surveillance of all known crime luminaries in the area—and there were plenty of those—with the jaws of a massive police trap set and ready to spring the moment another Bolan "hit" materialized.

"It is our chief advantage," said Skipper Garvey, "that we know most if not all of the probable targets. By concentrating surveillance on these known elements, we narrow the field of police detection and increase the probability of direct contact with the subject. This is our chief advantage."

Holzer muttered, "It's also our chief shame. If we know them, why the hell are they running around loose?"

"Knowing is not touching, John," replied the cynic at his elbow. "I gave up trying years ago, about the time they pinned the ass's tail on Pimlico." The reference was to a former Detroit police crusader.

"Nobody pinned no tail on George Pimlico," Holzer argued.

"Then why's he tucked safely away in Lansing

instead of busting their asses on the streets of Detroit?" the guy sneered.

"That was a kick upstairs and you know it," Holzer said.

"How many convictions has he gotten from Lansing?"

"More than he ever got around here, bet your ass."

"You still can't touch those people, John. You just can't touch them."

"Tell that," Holzer snarled, "to Mack Bolan!"

The meeting was over, and had deteriorated into clutch groups rehashing the Alert Plan. Holzer pushed angrily out of the group at his table and beat it to the relatively clean air of the corridor.

Tim Rossiter, a young sergeant from his home detail, awaited him there. Rossiter came over with an owlish look to report, "Favorini checked himself out of the hospital at ten o'clock."

"Who's on him?"

"Powell and Chardan. He went straight back to his place in the Woods."

"Any movements yet?"

"Naw," Rossiter replied. "Just a lot of phone calls. He's calling in all his guns."

"Figures," Holzer said. "Okay. Let's keep a full crew on that guy. If anybody decides to go after Bolan, it will be Charley Fever. I, uh, will have to handle this by remote, Tim. I got the damned contingency unit on this Alert Plan."

"Contingency for what?"

"Full riot conditions. We're in full mobilization."

"What the hell!"

"You tell me," Holzer replied, grimacing. "Aw. Be fair, they have a right to be jumpy. A guy like Bolan can catalyze a lot of simmering pots. They just don't want anything getting out of hand."

"Hell, it's your case, Lieutenant," Rossiter complained. "What the hell do they mean putting you on—"

"Hey, it's everybody's case," Holzer said gruffly. "Anyway, it gives me more freedom this way. I can nose around everywhere." He jotted a series of radio frequencies on a note pad, tore off the sheet, and handed it to Rossiter. "These are the specials. Beat it back to the Pointe and get these capabilities plugged into your communications. I'll be spending the next twenty-four hours either right here or in my vehicle. Keep me advised."

"Will do." The sergeant grinned soberly and hurried away.

Holzer lit a cigarete and paced the corridor until he'd smoked it to his fingers, then he went back inside.

His "mad" was over. Why shouldn't a veteran cop get cynical? It was true. You really could *not* touch those cruds, except on wrist-slapping offenses.

But somebody could.

The guy had come.

And he was slapping more than wrists.

And, now, these same cynical cops were being asked to shoot that dude on sight, to treat him like a mad-dog psychopath—the sanest guy in town.

Yeah. It was a crazy world, Holzer's was. And he simply did not know what to do about it. But he'd a damn sight rather get *mad* than *cynical*. Cynicism was just another way of getting *bought*—and there was enough of those around, as it was.

Crazy, yeah. A hell of a crazy world.

Those who could not be *touched* were being used as bait to trap the one who could not be *seen*—so that the trapee could also not touch the *baitee* who could never become the *touchee* by an other apparent manner.

Crazy, sure. But it was the only world John Holzer had. And it just beat the pink frosted shit out of becoming the *boughtee*.

He returned to the bull room and found the place in chaos.

Holzer grabbed a harried uniformed officer and asked him, "What the hell is going on?"

"It's that damned guy!" the cop replied, marveling. "He just hit an assembly plant over near Willow Run!"

Holzer swore under his breath and hurried on to the operations center. The detail leaders were grouped about a command console, watching an automated display taking shape on an electronic deployment screen. Holzer nudged one of the men and quietly inquired, "What's the score?"

"Indians ten, cowboys zip," the guy growled.

"What happened?"

"Nobody really knows for sure, yet. A shop steward, guy named Kazini, was the apparent target. No one knows how Bolan got in or out. Suddenly he was there, and Kazini was suspended from a hook above a dip tank—screaming bloody murder. Security people arrived in force but the blue-collars mobbed them—neutralized them. Apparently

91

Bolan was in there for about ten minutes after that, talking to some of the workers. Then he disappeared."

"What about Kazini?" Holzer wondered.

"They hauled him down, safe and sound. Plant security contacted us and requested Federal Narcotics out there quick. And they shut down the final delivery line, quarantined all the finished vehicles on hand."

"What?"

"Yeah," the cop growled. "Sounds like a distribution point, huh. Pretty sweet, at that. How many million bucks worth of horse do you figure could be built into a new car?"

"The Canadian connection," Holzer muttered.

"Yeh. What a setup. What a damn sweet setup."

"Until Bolan," Holzer commented, frowning. "So what about him?"

"It looks too late. We're setting up checkpoints . . . but what the hell. The guy was long gone before we even got the report. I don't know about this guy, John. He's not buying our traps."

Holzer turned away, suppressing a grin.

Maybe it was not such a crazy world, at that. At least *one* guy didn't seem to be buying the idea. *Nor* the bait.

12: PINNED

As number two man in a Massachusetts crime family, Leo Turrin was the highest-placed undercover fed in the race. As if those two hats were not difficult enough to wear together, he was also the best living friend of Mack Bolan, a long-declared enemy of both of Leo Turrin's worlds. His voice, as it traveled across the long-distance telephone connection, was crackling with interest.

"They've got the deathwatch on you, Sarge. You caught me just as I was going out the door. I got orders straight from the commission to get my tail to Detroit with all possible haste. They even chartered me a jet. I'm bringing twenty guns with me. Hell, I don't know how many other fire teams are being sent in from other points. I do know that my plane is stopping at Buffalo to pick up a contingent from there."

"It figures," Bolan replied quietly.

"And that's just the dark side of the street,"

Turrin went on. "The entire tricounty area around Detroit is on alert. Those Detroit cops are very sensitive about crime in their streets. They've had their full share of troubles around there, you know, and they're not taking kindly to the craps game you've got started there. I called Brognola early this morning, soon as I heard about—"

"Where is he? Still in Texas?"

"Naw, but his storm troopers are. Picking up the pieces. Hal's back in Washington. He says about you, Sarge: for Christ's sake, cool it. He's going to have to start loading up with real slugs if you don't take a rest and lay low for a while. Argentina, he says, still looks nice."

"It always did," Bolan muttered. "The war is *here*, Leo."

"Yeah. Well. Don't blame Hal. He's up to his eyeballs in intrigue of his own. Washington is in disarray, you know that. Lack of public confidence and all that. Someone very high is lighting the fires under your cross, wants you caught or shot without further fucking around. Maybe it's just a diversion, but Hal is really on the hot seat. This goes a lot higher than the justice department, Sarge. I mean, you know, like the whole damned government is toppling—a certain branch of it, anyway. You know what Charlie Wilson had to say about General Motors."

"What's good is good, yeah."

"Translate that to Detroit, buddy, because it's all the same ball game anyway. What's good for Detroit is good for the country and vice versa. It seems we have a five star bellringer of an emergency shaping up for this country, and *no*body in

94

Washington wants to see a Bolan blitz ripping through the tenderloin of our economy."

"I'm not after the economy," Bolan said tiredly.

"Same difference, man. Who the hell do you think is controlling the economy in that area?"

"You don't really believe that, Leo."

"No, I don't, but there are those who do. There are those who say our system can't survive without illegal manipulation."

"Like who?"

"Well, like the people who worry about recession and inflation, the rise and fall of the dollar and the stock markets, the balance of power between labor and management, all that. Especially that last. The goddamn mob has a firmer grip on the workers in that town than the goddamn unions have. As rotten as that is, at least it's a grip. The planners are projecting unemployment figures like right out of your blowing mind, and they're saying that the fall of Detroit is going to be the shot heard 'round the world. It's going to be an implosion, with the whole technological world falling in on Detroit. They're saying—"

"Leo, wait. I don't have time for a social study."

Turrin chuckled.

"And I'm not buying that argument. If you're saying that corrupted shop stewards who push narcotics and operate numbers and vigorish concessions have a grip on the worker—then, yeah, I'll buy that, okay. A grip right around his balls, buddy."

"I told Hal I'd try," Turrin said. "So I tried."

"Okay. Try something for me. Who's the head whoremaster around this town?"

"That's a hard one to pin," Turrin replied. "Tony Quaso wore the name, but . . . well, you know . . ."

Bolan said, "Yeah. Give me an educated guess, Leo. Who was he wearing it for?"

"It's tough for old leopards to change their spots."

"Meaning what?"

"Meaning none of the old heads really change. They try to clean up their image with semilegit interests and all that, but . . . well, you know, Sarge. A pimp is a pimp, all the way to his grave."

"I guess I'm not really looking for a pimp," Bolan said thoughtfully. "Who's running the hottest semilegit action out of the area?"

"That would be industrials," Turrin replied promptly.

"Okay. Lecture me, Professor."

"You probably know most of the background," Turrin said. "Laundry facilities, let's say."

"Okay. Who's washing the most money, and how?"

"That would be Butch Cassidy."

"Bobby Cassiopea," Bolan translated.

"Right. He's franchised by the Combination. Converts their black money into negotiable securities, trades the securities for gilt-edge stocks, municipal bonds, and so forth, pyramids the whole thing into real estate holdings, hospitals, nursing homes—you name it, Butch Cassidy will buy it. A lot of cannibalization goes on. Quick profits, you know, at the expense of company stability. That money finds its way into Swiss accounts and back through into more acquisitions, mergers, another

96

round of cannibalization, then even higher levels of international business swindles."

"He was the guy behind International Bankers Holding," Bolan mused.

"That's the guy. Got his tail burned a bit on that one." Turrin laughed softly. "Thanks to a certain blitz artist I happen to call friend."

"Would you," Bolan mused on, "connect Cassiopea with an international jet set of party girls?"

"Sure," Turrin shot right back. "The guy operates in grand style. Entertains lavishly. Nothing's too good for a prospective pigeon about to be fleeced of his company or his factory or his brokerage house. And that goes double in spades for impressionable government officials or greedy heads of state. As for the girls, it's amazing how pitifully stupid a hardboiled businessman or politico can become over the prospect of some delectably forbidden free ass. Uh, Sarge. My wheelman's getting nervous, and I've run out of time."

"You gave me what I needed, Leo. Thanks."

"Wait a sec. You can leave messages for me at the Sheraton-Cadillac."

"Okay. That your headquarters here?"

"No, my drop. We'll probably be mobbed up somewhere. But I'll check the message desk at the hotel every four hours. Starting about mid-afternoon."

Bolan said, "Great. Watch your swinger, Leo." He hung up and returned to the vehicle, where Toby Ranger waited impatiently.

"Who were you talking to—God?" she groused.

"Closest thing to it I've found on earth," he replied, smiling.

She stared the engine and asked, "Where to now?"

"Central precinct," he said.

"What?" She put a foot on the brake and turned to him with a hard, searching gaze.

"You heard me," he said quietly.

"You're not dropping me and—!"

"Not you. Me."

"What?"

"Toby. Take me to Central. I have business there."

"You're insane!"

"Maybe so, but take me anyway."

"Captain Crazy," she muttered, dazed and still not sure how she should respond to the insane command.

"Take your foot off the brake, Toby. Give the wheel a small spin left, gradually depress the accelerator and—"

"Oh, shut up!"

He was grinning at her, adding fuel to the flames.

She moved on into the flow of traffic and edged left for the swing onto Woodward. Her eyes were popping sparks in all directions, and the atmosphere inside the car fairly quivered with suppressed tensions by the time they arrived at the destination and she pulled into the area reserved for police vehicles.

"Whatever you have to do here, let me do it," she said, in a voice just barely under control.

"Go back to the apartment," he commanded firmly. "Wait for my call. I'm going to need you, Toby. Both of us will."

"Both of who?" she asked, the control slipping and her voice breaking.

"The Canuck and I," he said, and kissed her quickly, and got out of there.

He walked straight into the official entrance, and she watched him disappear into that ominous interior.

Then she wheeled the car around and sped away from there, half-blinded by a sudden gush of tears.

"Damn you," she whispered. "Just damn you all the way back to me in one piece."

It was a prayer, couched in reverse English—and, it seemed at that moment, a terribly forlorn one.

13: STRUCK

A tall guy with an open watch book in hand was moving gracefully about the strike room, talking in earnest with members of the task force, studying the postings and making notes as the hard, detail work of police methodology continued along its grinding course.

The guy walked past John Holzer, locked eyes momentarily, smiled, and went on for a closer look at the contingency postings.

Holzer asked one of his people, "Who is that guy?"

"Hell, I don't know," the cop replied. "We got cops here from everywhere, places I never knew existed until this morning."

"I know him from somewhere."

"Ask him."

"I will."

But the guy had moved on. Holzer followed with his gaze and saw him walk into the federal area, shake hands with a strike force fed, then move into the stake-outs section.

Holzer ambled over and asked the fed, "Who is that guy?"

"Which guy?"

"You just shook his hand. He went into the tac room."

"Oh. That's Stryker. Spell it with a *y*."

"One of your people, eh."

"I think so."

"You *think* so."

"That's what I said," the fed replied, a bit testily.

"Well, what is that, a code name or something?" the lieutenant from Grosse Pointe persisted. "I mean, *strike* force? *Stryker?*"

"I don't know what you're getting at," the fed said, definitely testy now. "Go play games with someone else. I'm busy."

The guy was reading the morning paper. Holzer said, "Yeah, you look busy," and passed on to the tac room.

The tall guy was talking to a vice squad lieutenant, pointing out something on one of the big city grid maps that choked the walls of the place. The vice man was shaking his head and stabbing a finger into another area of the chart. They were having a pretty good argument when the tall guy gazed over the other man's head and directly into Holzer's eyes. Something sparked there, and he raised a hand and crooked a finger. It could not have been meant for anyone else; Holzer pursed his lips and stepped forward.

The tall guy said, "Let's see, it's John Holzer, isn't it? Grosse Pointe?"

Holzer nodded. "And you're—"

"Do you know Lieutenant Kelso here? DPD Vice."

The two lieutenants locked eyes and nodded. "We've met," Kelso said with evident irritation.

"Policeman's Ball, maybe," Holzer said sarcastically.

"You got vice up there, Holzer," Kelso growled. "You got half the goddamn mob up there."

"Three-fourths," Holzer replied amiably. He wished he could place the tall dude in his mind.

But the tall dude was placing something else in John Holzer's mind. "Kelso says the Eight Mile triangle between East Detroit and Harper Woods has been cleaned out, neutralized."

"You mean that area up there opposite the high school complex," Holzer said, glancing at the wall chart.

"Exactly," Kelso growled. "They got three high schools side by side there—they got Notre Dame, Regina, and Lutheran East."

"But they're in Harper Woods," the tall man said.

"So what? They were screaming like hell because of—and that's why I'm saying it's clean as a hound's tooth, the whole Detroit triangle from Kelley to Hayes and up to Eight Mile. We sweep that area once a week, and I'm telling you, it's clean."

"That's close to your area, Holzer," the tall dude said quietly. "Do you agree with that?"

"Not exactly," Holzer said.

"Aw, *bull*," the Vice lieutenant exploded. "You name one joint that we missed, just one!"

Holzer stretched to tap the chart. "How about Linda's Salon? She was operating full blast last time I passed there. Couple days ago."

Kelso was glaring at the grid map. "What's that again now?"

"Linda just happens to be Palooka Joe Venedetti's sister-in-law. You know what Palooka Joe deals in, Kelso?"

"Where is that? Show me where that is!"

The lieutenant from Grosse Pointe busied himself at the chart for a moment. He was aware that the tall guy had squeezed past his shoulder, but he did not miss the guy until he looked up from the brief task—and the guy was gone again.

Kelso had snatched up a plastic overlay sheet and was posting the stake-out board with the new intelligence. "Okay," he growled to Holzer. "It goes on, at least 'til I can check it out. You better —what's the matter, Holzer? You look like you just saw a ghost or something."

"Who is that guy, Kelso?"

"Who—the big guy? Thought *you* knew. Hell, he introduced you."

"Yeah, but who introduced *him?*" Holzer wondered in a chocked voice. He went out of there without another word to the man from Vice and hurried into the strike room.

The fed with the newspaper glanced up, then went back to his reading. "Stryker come back through here?" Holzer demanded.

"You've got a complex, mister," the fed said, and that's all he said.

103

Holzer had *something* as he hurried on across the large room and through the babble of organized confusion, but it wasn't a complex. It was a shaking gut and the certain sinking conviction that he had finally "placed" the tall man in his mental mug file.

But, hell, surely it couldn't be. *No* guy would try *that*. No guy in his right mind would stroll right into the enemy's war room, peer over the shoulders of the general staff, and engage them in debates on strategy and tactics.

No guy—well, okay, maybe one guy would. Maybe he would, at that. Some guys just worked harder, and that's why they worked better.

All the same, John Holzer was going to feel like the chump of the century if it turned out to be—if he'd actually been standing there talking to—hell, puppy-dogging the guy all over the damn place . . . oh, *God!*

He found the make sheets and went through them one by one—front view, profile left, profile right . . . hell, it *could* be. Artist's conceptions weren't all that great, not all the time—a composite sketch depended a lot on the reliability of the witness's observational powers. But, yeah, it *could be* the guy!

He dropped the sheets and ran to the corridor, dying a little with each pace of the trip.

The guy *called him by name—knew* him! How'd he get that? The same way, maybe, that Holzer got "Stryker"? By just simply asking somebody?

What did the guy have, for God's sake, a photoelectric mind? Could he walk into a strike room

104

like that, casually look it over, and walk away with the entire counterplan blazed across his brains?

If Holzer couldn't *find* the guy—if he couldn't nail him and make him produce proper identification—what then? What could he do? Run to the skipper and tell him to change the game? Just because a kid lieutenant from Grosse Pointe thought he'd entertained Mack Bolan unawares in watch headquarters?

Holzer ran to the main lobby and on through to the outside, spent thirty seconds or so in a visual search there, then reversed course and ran through to the vehicle area.

There was not a sign of the guy, not anywhere.

So . . . what now, Holzer?

Nothing, that was what. Who'd believe it, anyway?

But he *knew* the guy now, knew what he looked like, knew how he walked and moved and held his head, knew the sound of his voice and the flash of those remarkable eyes. Yeah. No introduction would be necessary the next time.

Stryker, eh?

The knot in John Holzer's belly melted, and he found himself laughing inside.

The Metro Unified Strike Force had become the struckee. Supernatural, no. Supermilitary—yeah, hell, yeah!

And crazy, sure, like a fox.

14: CONDITIONED

Since that first desperate battle at Pittsfield, Bolan had been conditioning his survival instincts for the inevitable armed confrontation that must someday occur between himself and the law.

It was a negative conditioning.

Cops were just people, sure—no better and no worse than most. The greater number of the ones he's run into were pretty good—decent guys struggling to do their job well, husbands and fathers doing their best with family responsibilities, professional soldiers with a hell of a thankless task and uncertain destinies.

A cop played the game of survival every time he hung a gun and donned the badge. It was a necessary game for a species of planetary life that had learned to think and act for itself but not to discipline itself.

Most people even disliked the sound of the word: discipline.

So, sure, cops were necessary if men were to live together in a responsible and disciplined society.

Mack Bolan was not at war with those men in blue—even if nobody knew that but himself. It was their job to enforce the law. Bolan was breaking it. Bolan was out of step, not them. He had never disliked a man for doing his duty as he understood it.

Bolan would not kill a cop. The war wasn't worth that. The war involved more than simply wiping out rattlesnakes. There existed a deeper plane—a *primum mobile,* or prime mover—that said that *right* had to triumph over *wrong.*

There was no way to cut it and say that it was *right* to shoot a cop. No personalities involved, no good or bad guy consciousness at stake, that badge of law was a symbol of freedom in a society of equals. This was Bolan's understanding. The badge proclaimed that the law of the jungle did not rule here, that men of reason had come together to fashion and hold a responsible society, that the jungle would not be allowed to encroach upon that clearing.

The man wearing the badge patrolled that jungle, of course, and sometimes he fell victim to it. Crooked cops were simply another testament to the imperfection of man. The man could not debase the badge, however; the badge itself was a perfect idea, and it merited respect from those who sought its protection—from those who wished to live *outside the jungle.*

Bolan, waging war from that deeper dimension, the *primum mobile,* would not shoot at such a symbol of *right*. And so the conditioning, the *negative* approach to the strongest instinct within a warrior's breast—that problem of survival.

In the jungle, a threatened entity did not pause to intellectualize his predicament. He reacted instinctively—with either fight or flight. With flight impossible, the cornered beast would struggle to the death, utilizing every fang and claw at his disposal.

And this was what worried Bolan, the man. He did not desire that the warrior survive an armed confrontation with the badge. He would exhaust every possibility of *flight* within reach, but when the corners closed about him, he wanted to be certain that all fangs and claws of the survival instinct knew when to draw back, lie down, and die.

Without, perhaps, calling it that, Bolan consciously cultivated an overlying *death* instinct—an innate self-destruct switch to open the grave and fill it with Mack Bolan's personal war.

He was going to die, anyway, eventually. He would not die with friendly blood on his hands.

He would not kill a soldier of the same side.

The only option, if the war was to continue, was to *evade* them. *Evade* and *hide* are not synonymous terms. There were times when, in order to properly *evade* the cops, it was necessary that he walk among them.

The penetration of the strike headquarters at Detroit Central was such an exercise

He needed to know what the soldiers in blue were up to. He had to know where and how to move across that jungle of survival that they all trod, without confrontation. And he especially wished to know if they were watching a particular section of jungle that the Executioner strongly desired to invade.

And they were.

Even though Bobby Cassiopea had enjoyed an extremely low profile in Mafia circles, he was now on their list. It had been only very recently that even the federal specialists had begun to suspect this "international financier" as a front for the ganglords.

A reluctant fed must have wrung his conscience hard over that one. Cassiopea represented a lot of potential dynamite. To put his name on a local list and risk the loss of a very quiet federal investigation showed, to Bolan's mind, the desire those same feds had for Bolan himself. It was not exactly a comforting thought.

The "quiet watch" on Cassiopea was perfectly understandable. Bolan could sympathize with Brognola and others in the national headshed who were uneasy about playing dice with the fate of a dozen or more multinational conglomerates—especially at such a time in this country's troubled flirtations with economic disaster.

The "energy problem" was no more than the tip of an iceberg encountered by Bolan very briefly in Texas. Beneath that floating projection lay an entire subcontinent of international enganglements and potential earth-shakers that, sure, could make even an economic giant like the United States tremble and perhaps even topple.

Cassiopea was not a hood—not in the usual

sense. He held a law degree from a prestigious midwestern school and was a recognized authority on international business law. In a write-up in *Newsweek*, once, he had been described as "the golden boy of international finance" and, in a more personal vein, "the playboy financier of the western world."

Only once had the guy been even remotely connected publicly with shady business tactics, and this involved a penny-ante securities swindle in Utah some years back. Even here, though, Cassiopea had managed to convince everyone concern that he had been duped along with the other victims.

According to Bolan's poop sheet, the guy was forty-one years of age, married to, but living apart from, a genuine Italian countess, had two youngsters who spent most of their lives in European boarding schools.

He owned a joint in Grosse Pointe Woods—not far from the mob's yacht club. He kept offices downtown, not far from civic center, and had a "retreat" up near Bald Mountain between Pontiac and Flint.

At one of those spots, or upon some jungle trail connecting them, Bolan expected to discover the key to the riddle of Georgette Chableu's fate.

Let the earth shake where it would, there came a time for every man when he had to stand down from the impersonal war and deal entirely on the people level.

Georgette was special people.

Somehow Bolan had to isolate Cassiopea from

those who watched and waited, maneuver him into a section of unpatrolled "jungle," and pin an Executioner badge on the guy.

Somehow. Yeah. But how?

15: COUNTED

Bolan proceeded directly from the strike room to the police garage. Pool vehicles were being serviced there and put on the line with the special strike net radio frequencies plugged in. It was a routine operation made difficult only by the quantity of vehicles involved.

The master of "role camouflage" needed one of those vehicles.

His senses flared into the situation and unerringly focused upon the service boss, a harried man in his middle years with too much to do and too little to do it with.

Bolan possessed a special knack for getting "in step" with people. Perhaps it was one of the secrets of his success.

He approached the service boss with a sympathetic grin and told him, "Don't rush, just get it done yesterday, eh?"

The guy grinned back, sourly, and replied,

"Same old shit. When it gets this bad, I stop worrying. It can only get better."

Bolan chuckled. "Maybe not. I could be coming down here to tell you the game's changed again. Take it all out and put it back like it was."

The guy's grin faded. He muttered, "Is it?"

Bolan laughed again and playfully poked the guy's shoulder. "Nah. No time for cheap jokes, is it?" He handed over a business card that had thoughtfully been handed to him in the strike room. "Skipper wants you to check your list for this guy. Make sure he's on it."

The service boss accepted the card and frowned at it. "Why don't the feds furnish these vehicles?" he complained. "If they're going to send the man, they should send the car with him."

Bolan shrugged. "You know how it is during a flap. Hey, we don't want to send the guy over to Avis—right? Detroit tries harder because we're only number three—right?"

The guy laughed. "Well . . ."

"He *is* on the list, huh?"

"Naw." A tired sigh. "But he will be."

"I should pick up the car right now. This is, uh, you know, one of those protocol things. Skipper doesn't want these guys going back telling tales out of school."

"Yeah," the guy growled. Now he was being sympathetic. "Same old shit." He was scanning a log book. "Okay." He spun the book around and indicated a line with his finger. "This one's ready."

Bolan accepted a ball-point pen and scribbled a badge number in the space provided. "Thanks. Remind me to buy you a beer."

113

"Buy me a couple more mechanics instead."

Bolan laughed and looked toward the vehicles. "Head of the line, eh?"

"Right. Gassed and ready. That one just had a brake job. If it pulls a little, let the self-adjustors burn in."

Bolan thanked the guy again and went to claim his vehicle. It was fairly new, unmarked, with an inconspicuous antenna. Perfect. He slid in, cranked it, checked the radio, and checked the hell out of there.

The plan was only vaguely formed in his mind, but he knew what he had to do. *How* he would do it remained to be seen.

Off the numbers now and by the ear, the Executioner was again on the offensive. Let friends and enemies stand up and be counted. The jungle would claim her own.

Officers Larson and Papado were two short hours into their vigil and just beginning to settle into the tedium of a long stake-out.

They were positioned for surveillance of the main entrance to the Cadillac Tower Building, with a third detective stationed in the lobby and in direct radio communications with the vehicle.

Blown-up photos of one Bobby Cassiopea, lifted from a magazine and a couple of old newspapers, lay on the seat between the two men, sharing honors with composite sketches of the man of the moment, Mack Bolan.

Larson uncorked a thermos of coffee and poured a slug into a paper cup. "Want some?" he asked his partner.

114

Papado responded with a negative grunt, then added, "My ass is going dead."

"Shift to the other cheek," Larson suggested.

"I've run out of cheeks."

"Play with your balls or something. That'll get the blood to pumping again."

Papado chuckled. "What we need on these gigs is female partners. I'd feel self-conscious playing with my own."

Larson sipped his coffee, then swiftly lowered the cup. "Get a look at that guy?"

"Yeah. Right build but too old."

"Better check him anyway."

Papado sighed and spoke into a small transistor radio. "Paul. Close-sight an incoming."

The response crackled back immediately. "Right."

A moment later, "Strike three, you're out."

Larson grimaced.

Papado sighed.

The watch went on. Both men rubbed their eyes and stretched their necks, repeatedly. Papado cracked his knuckles, cast an apologetic glance at his partner, separated his hands, shifted his position on the seat.

"Police work," Larson muttered ten minutes later. "The glamor of it all is damn near overpowering, isn't it? I'll end up with bifocals, barnacles on my ass, jock itch clear to my knees, and the ringing cry of 'Pig!' on my tombstone. Why, Pappy? Why the hell do we do it?"

Papado shrugged. "It's a living."

"So's playing tennis. Or golf. For God's sake, why *this?*"

His partner sighed. "We have to get into that again?"

A moment later, Larson said, "Sandy wants a divorce."

"Smart girl," Papado commented.

"I'm serious. She's at the ultimatum stage. I have to choose between her and the force."

"Too bad. You're going to miss that girl, Chuck."

"Get serious."

"I'm always serious."

"We're just not making it. Financially, I mean. Hell, we just worry through from one payday to the next, juggling bills, dodging them sometimes. Have you been grocery shopping lately? Hell . . . I don't know, Pappy."

"You don't know what?"

"We can't touch those bastards, anyway."

"What's that supposed to mean?"

Larson muttered, "May as well take their envelopes."

"Oh, boy," Papado said heavily. "I'm going to let you have one right in the mouth."

"Shit," Larson said.

"That's it exactly. Rub it all over you, why don't you? Eat some, too. That'll make you feel a lot better, won't it? Listen. I'd let my wife sell her ass first."

"I don't know, Pappy. I just don't know."

"Then take it from one that does. I grew up with that shit. You take their envelopes, buddy, then it's fair trade. They take your trembling immortal soul and use it for ass wipe. Look, I don't

116

even want to talk about this. Now I just don't want to talk about it. You reading me?"

"I'm reading you." A moment later: "Pappy, I was just bellyaching."

"I know it."

"Next time, go ahead. *Do* let me have one in the mouth."

"I probably will."

The partners lapsed into another silence.

Cops on stake-out duty had a lot of time to do nothing but think. It was perhaps their chief enemy.

A few minutes later their vehicle radio began making noises. "Strike Cadillac. This is Strike Seven Honcho."

Larson's eyes leapt along the communications bulletin. "That's the roving detail leader," he told his partner. "Delta channel."

Papado punched a button on the radio and grabbed the mike.

"Go ahead, Honcho Seven."

"Activity report."

Papado rolled eyes at his partner and replied, "Negative. No come, no go."

"Any contact with your surveillance subject?"

"Negative. Insider reports he is not logged in, repeat, not on premises."

"Okay. The whole horseshoe is quiet. Spell each other for a break. But stay close."

"Roger. Thanks."

Papado returned the mike to its bracket and told Larson, "I thought the roving detail didn't start 'til dark."

The other officer shrugged. "They change the game every five minutes. You want to eat first?"

"Too early. But I'd like to air my ass. Walk around the block, maybe."

Larson chuckled. "Okay. Go ahead. Don't pick up any stray envelopes."

Papado took a playful swing at his partner's chin, stepped out of the vehicle, then leaned back in to say, "Don't *you* pick up any stray Executioners. Save them 'til I get back."

"Never worry," Larson replied to that. "I'd bet a tenner the guy isn't within fifty miles of here."

The bored detective would have lost his bet.

"The guy"—most recently known as "Strike Seven Honcho"—had just cruised them at a distance of fifty yards.

Some minutes and some miles farther along, another patiently bored officer on the quietest duty of all completed an activity check with "Strike Nine Honcho" and turned to his partner with a sigh. "You ever get the feeling," he asked, "that the watchers are always being watched? That was a strong signal. I'll bet he was looking at us all the time we were talking."

The other man shrugged and fed in another stick of gum to sweeten the tension-relieving cud. "Whole town's uptight," he commented. "You want to play the game, you take the cards they deal you."

"I just don't like playing the game with a joker in the deck."

"Roving Leader is no joker. We get a positive contact, you'll be damn glad that guy's out there somewhere to back you up."

118

"I hear Bolan doesn't shoot at cops."

"Maybe true. Maybe not. How's he going to know you're a cop? You got it tatooed across your forehead with neon ink?"

The patrolman chuckled nervously. "Maybe you're right. The rovers weren't due on until night shift. I guess this really is a Mad Dog alert."

"Right. A guy comes busting up, shooting and throwing explosives, he doesn't write any names on it. You just can't call shots in a game like that guy plays, Jack. You can't call them. Right?"

"Yeah, right, I guess so. Right."

Wrong.

The "Strike Honcho" of the unofficial day watch was indeed writing names and calling shots.

It was the name of his game—the only game he cared to play.

16: SHIVERED

John Holzer was a cop who trusted his instincts. In the final analysis, according to Holzer, effective police work relied at least fifty percent on the intuitive process, with or without all the fancy technology that had been plugged into the war against crime. A cop who could not react to spinal shivers was only about half cop.

And Lieutenant Holzer had been fighting the shivers for a full twenty minutes. He finally gave it up and went into the tac room for a word with Joe Daley, an inspector with thirty years under his belt. Daley had been the long route with the Detroit force, from beat cop up through the ranks and now he was a candidate for promotion to district inspector. At the moment, he was the watch commander for the special strike force alert. He'd been a friend of Holzer's father, a good cop who'd died with his badge on some years back.

"You've got the look," Daley intoned somberly,

"of a pup that went out to tree a bear and found himself up the tree and alone. Don't like your detail?"

"It's okay," Holzer told the old family friend. "Tell me something, Joe. What do your shivers tell you about this case?"

"They're not talking to me yet."

"No?"

"No. But yours are, I guess."

The inspector picked up a phone and said a few crisp words into it. Holzer held his tongue and fidgeted, his gaze roaming over the wall displays.

Daley hung up the phone and told his young friend, "Look, the guy hit your beat first. I can understand how you feel. You have a territorial claim. Okay. But a good cop—"

"It isn't that, Joe. It's . . . well . . . either I've completely flipped or I was talking to that guy a little while ago."

Shrewd eyes measured the youngster. "Yeah? Where?"

Holzer's gaze swerved left. "Right over there."

"Right over where?"

"Just about where Kelso is standing right now."

"I thought we were talking about Bolan."

Holzer swallowed and said, "That's the one."

Joe Daley scratched his cheek. "And when was this?"

The lieutenant from Grosse Pointe consulted his watch. "Thirty minutes ago."

"Why didn't you say something then?"

"The guy had vanished by the time my shivers stared talking sense."

"And when was that?"

121

Holzer made a wry face. "Just about the moment he disappeared. I looked for him. Ran through the building like a loony searching for him. No catch."

Daley commented, "And still no speak until now. Why not?"

"Do you always speak your shivers right off, Joe?"

"If it seems appropriate. Just what are you telling me, Johnny? Are you saying the guy came in and looked us over? He walked right into a police station, somehow found the right office out of a hundred possibles, cased the joint, and walked out? Without anyone in the place recognizing him—except you?"

"Yeah. Yeah." Holzer bunched his shoulders and gazed at the wall.

"Why would he do that?"

"That's what I've been wondering for the past thirty minutes. Aw, damn it, Joe. Look at the record on this guy! He's made monkeys out of every force in the country. The feds have been chasing him from hell to breakfast ever since his first hit. Not only that but every hood in the country who can scrape up the price of a Saturday night special is dreaming of collecting bounty on the guy. The mob has been fielding special head units from the word go. But he just strolls blithely through it all. How? How does he do that? We can't even get a decent artist's composite! What the hell does he really look like? Are cops *really* turning their heads when he passes by, or is it just that they don't even know the guy is there? There has to be some explanation for—"

"Hey cool it, hold it there! In one-syllable words, exactly what the hell are you telling me, Johnny?"

"That's the hell of it, I just don't know," Holzer admitted miserably. "Except . . . damnit, I *know* the guy was in here. And . . ."

"Yeah?"

"It doesn't seem to be a *police* case, Joe."

"What is it, then?"

"I don't know what it *is*. I know what it's *not*. Look. Police methods are geared to the apprehension of criminals."

"Whoever said they weren't? And whoever said Mack Bolan was anything but a criminal?"

"That's just it. You've hit it right there, Joe. It's why the guy comes and goes as he damn pleases. Wrong *methods*, Joe. Damnit, we're going about it all wrong."

"You're a cop, Johnny."

"Right, I am."

"Your old man was a cop. *I'm* a cop. Every man in this damn *room* is a cop. Now, how should we go about our jobs? What *method* should we be using?"

"This guy is militating us."

"He's what?"

"All right, maybe I used the wrong word. But this guy's a *soldier*. He's fighting a *war*, damn it. It is *not* a gang war—not in the sense we think of gang wars. And he's not fighting *us*. He's fighting *them*."

"So? Go on."

Several detectives were standing in the back-

123

ground, listening with interest to the conversation at Daley's desk.

Holzer shot a glance at the men behind him and went doggedly on. "The guy was in here, Joe. He walked around the strike room for ten minutes or more, talking to everybody, reading the postings, taking notes. I thought he was some cop I knew from somewhere. I guess everybody else who thought anything at all had the same impression. But somehow my interest showed more than anybody else's. He caught that, Joe. He caught it right off, knew I was *wondering*. He split quick then, and I tagged him into this room. He'd gone up to Kelso and shook him with some uncomplimentary observation. Kelso was debating the guy. The guy saw me coming after him. He picked my name off somewhere and hit me with it. Quick, oh boy, smooth and quick, and he worked me to a final sigh, let me tell you. Even got me to arguing with Kelso, then he simply faded away. Now, Joe—tell me something—have you ever known a hood or any other criminal type who could get away with something like that?"

The old cop was thinking about it. He sighed and came to his feet. "How many times," he asked ponderously, "have you damn near hung a man with a thin-air case like that one? You expect me to go to the skipper with a Swiss cheese hypothesis like this? There's more holes than facts. It probably *was* a cop you knew from somewhere. We got guys coming in here every five minutes. We got another planeload of feds due in most any minute. They swarm to this Bolan guy like bees to

124

a honeycomb. It's like a police convention around here. We got—"

"Joe, damn it—Inspector—I went back and studied the composites. They're close. Damned close. And my hackles have been yelling at me ever since."

"Well, get out of here with your hackles," Daley said gruffly. He caught the agony in the young cop's eyes and added, "Look, you're a good cop. I wouldn't take that away from you, Holzer. But hell, we're all jumpy today. Instincts can be wrong as hell, especially when we're leaping at every shadow. Based on what you've told me, I'm not going to go to the skipper and tell him that the man who caused this massive mobilization of very expensive police manpower casually dropped in to hobnob and swap ideas while we labored on with the *dragnet* for the guy. I'm not going to do that, Holzer. So you get out of here, get back to your own detail, and take your shivers with you."

Someone in the background chuckled.

Holzer opened his mouth and closed it, then spun blindly away in angered defeat.

He bounced off another officer who had just hurried over for a piece of the watch commander's attention.

"Inspector," the guy announced worriedly, "we have something funny going on in Communications."

Holzer froze and cocked his ear.

"What now?" Daley asked disgustedly.

"The roving details start with the night watch —right? There's been no change in that?"

125

"No change," Daley growled. "You don't need those communications until—"

"That's just it. The strike dispatcher accidentally turned on the delta channel monitor, and he heard a roving leader talking to a stake-out detail up in Harper Woods. I got to checking. Two other disricts report radio contacts with roving leaders. That's in Strike 7, Strike 8, and Strike 9."

Holzer had moved back into position at Daley's desk, listening with interest to the report.

The watch commander was staring at the man from Communications with eyes narrowed to mere peep-slits.

Holzer coughed delicately and said, "Are your shivers talking to you now, Joe?"

17: FATED

"Glad you caught the coder," Leo Turrin's taut tones greeted the Executioner. "This is very hot."

"And getting hotter," Bolan said. "I've been wanting to spot you. Where's that phone booth, Leo?"

"Just down the street from Tommy Damio's place. That's our headquarters, please take note. You're a couple minutes late. I was about to go on."

"Sorry. I've been busy. Just got the message. What's so hot?"

"Brognola."

Bolan said, "Tell Hal—"

"No wait! Hear mine first. This is really hot, straight from the headshed. Hal says scratch all past favors, scratch everything. He's putting it right on the line this time. This is tough, so hear me out. He says, quote: 'Do not even breathe upon the person or the mere shadow of Butch Cassidy,' unquote. It's an order. He wants you to understand that."

Bolan replied quietly, "Since when does the fed give me orders."

"Not your orders, buddy—*his*, straight from the oval office, I understand."

Bolan pondered that bit of information for a moment, then said, "It's that grave, eh?"

"Worse than grave, Sarge. Those guys in DC don't even breathe the name Cassiopea. They still use the code name, Butch Cassidy, in all references to the guy. The dirt they're digging up gets more frightening with every bite of the shovel. There are ramifications here so downright scary that they—"

Bolan interrupted with a terse, "Okay, Leo. Tell Brognola I'll try to not bruise the guy. But I *am* going to have a talk with him."

"No, Sarge—no. Not even that."

"Sorry, but I've got priorities too, Leo. I'm talking to the guy."

Turrin's voice was choked with defeat. "I know better than to argue with you. I trust your feel, Sarge. But for God's sake, the fed doesn't even want this guy to know that *they* know."

"They've got him on the make list here in Detroit."

"How do you know that?"

"He's staked out."

Turrin groaned.

Bolan said, "Don't worry about it. They're being very soft. Enough so that I believe I can slip through without a fuss."

"Watch yourself. Don't believe everything you

128

may have read about cops in Detroit. They're tough cookies, and they crumble with great difficulty."

"Yeah," Bolan agreed. "I got that reading. Well, my numbers are falling. Be dark soon. You're staying at Damio's all night?"

"Right, and don't ring off yet. I've got some intel for you. Something's not exactly on key here in mobtown. Charley Fever is beating the drums and getting all the old guard out to that joint you hit last night. I get the feeling that he's taking over. That's quite a step for a guy like Charley. I mean —he's plenty tough, sure. Right now he's walking around with a hole in his shoulder you could fish through. But he's never been anything more than a reliable gun hand—I guess you know that. He's coming on as the strong man now, though, and the old bosses are listening to him."

"So they're mobbing up at the hardsite?"

"Yeah. But just the old guard. This could be the crack we've been looking for all these years. Detroit has always been a very solid town, you know. I mean, no family intrigues. Well, here's the interesting part. I told you the old men back east were sending in head parties. That's about a dozen of them in town now, from almost any point you want to name. I get it now that there has been a fissure brewing here, just beneath the surface, for some time. Detroit never really stood close to the nationals, you know that. Apparently this has been due mainly to the influence of Crazy Sal. Well, now Sal is dead and—"

"He didn't make it, then?"

"Figured you knew. No. He died about noon today. Anyway, with Sal out of the picture, I believe the old men from the east hope to swing Detroit closer into the fold. Now Charley Fever, as I understand it, is rallying the old guard. The others have been very discreetly advised by *La Commissione* to stand clear of Charley Fever. Let him take the Bolan heat, they're saying. We're sending you guns to keep you insulated. Sit tight. And let Charley Fever worry about Mack Bolan."

Bolan grunted. "I could have written that script."

"Yeah. Well, it's a good one, from our point of view. You did some good work out there last night, Sarge, and Brognola wants you to know that he's well aware of it. It shook them good and embarrassed a lot of their traveling companions. Nobody got booked out there last night, but a hell of a lot of interesting names got added to the make lists. Now the whole Combination is jittery as hell. Hal would sure like it better, though, if you could just forget you ever heard of Butch Cassidy. I'm sorry I even mentioned the name."

"You didn't have to, Leo. And I can't forget it. It's a personal matter. I'll walk as softly as possible, but I have to make that guy."

Turrin sighed. "Then we'll consider him made. Talk to the guy if you feel like you must, but I got a personal message for you from myself."

"I'm listening."

"End it there. Talk to Butch Cassidy, find out whatever it is you think you have to know. Then fade. Quick. Go somewhere far and quiet, and lay for a while. This is between buddies. As you are standing there right now, Sarge, you're a dead

130

man. You're dead. Unless you get out of this town quick. Now they're up for you. All of them. Both sides of the street. The cops are at full mobe, riot units and all. By sundown they'll have roving patrols—you could call them destroyer forces—just prowling the streets and poised for a quick response. They have armored vehicles, massive firepower, gas, gadgets, the whole bit. Besides that, a special force of U.S. marshals hit town about an hour ago—every one of them an expert marksman and they're packing big rifles."

"I know about all that," Bolan commented wearily. "Thanks anyway."

"That's just one side. The other is just as bad. The cream of the country's streets have packed this town, and they're all heavy guns. I'm at Damio's, and holding. Buffalo is over at Thomasetta's. Three New York crews are brooding over—"

"Save it, Leo. I know."

"You save it. Get out."

"Can't."

"Damn it, why not? What's so damned urgent?"

"I told you. Personal."

"Graves are very impersonal, Sarge. What do you want engraved on your marker? 'Here lies Mack Bolan's war'? Over some personal vendetta?"

"It's no vendetta. It's an onus."

"A what?

"Forget it. I'll fade as soon as I can."

"Don't hit that joint out there again."

"The yacht club?"

"That's the one. They're expecting you back. Charley is stacking the joint with every gun he can command. It won't be as soft as it was last night."

"Who says it was soft last night?" Bolan muttered.

"Okay, call it piss hard for tonight. And stay away."

"I plan to."

"Okay. Hey. Don't get down on Hal. Hell, he's got high rankers crawling all over him."

"I know that," Bolan said. He sighed. "Brognola's a good man. Give him my best. But no apologies. I do what I have to do, Leo."

"Sure. Stay hard, man."

"You, too."

Bolan hung up, gazed coolly at the police vehicle parked alongside the booth, then thumbed in another dime. It was time to activate his auxiliary.

Her voice came on the line cool and calm. "Yes?"

"It's the guy," he told her. "You'll find keys in the coffee can. They fit a gray EconoLine van parked below, slot G-12. Pick me up at the corner of Kelly and Morang. Twenty minutes."

"Wait. Where's that? Approximately."

"East on Eight Mile to Kelly. That's just beyond Gratiot. South to Morang."

"Got it. Do you need the stuff in the other car?"

"I transferred it this morning."

"Oh, okay. Anything else?"

"Just be there."

"Try and keep me away," she replied breathlessly.

He hung up and watched the setting sun for a moment, then returned to the vehicle.

Sunrise, sunset. Birth, death. Man, woman. Person, cosmos. Yeah.

He lit a cigarette and put the car in motion.

All the numbers were in. The *onus* was in the saddle and riding Bolan. And the death image over Detroit was settling in for the night watch.

18: RIDDEN

Emerson had once observed, "Things are in the saddle, and ride mankind."

Bolan would not argue with a man so wise. He'd had the same feeling himself, many times.

He was already twelve hours beyond his deadline for leaving this town. The plan had been the usual—*hit* and *git*. Before the opposition could rally itself. Before the cops could gear up. Before the whirlpool of uncontrollable events could suck a guy into his grave.

Bolan's cosmic contempt was for *death*—not for life. He respected life and her myriad involvements. He was not exactly in love with the one he'd lived for the past few eternities—no man could truly enjoy a trip down blood river. Bolan certainly did not. But it was the only trip open to him now, his only apparent reason to go on living. And Mack Bolan certainly respected life enough to go on living, for as long as the grim game could be continued.

Sure, *things* were in the saddle. And they rode Bolan.

He had scouted this town with all the expertise at his disposal. He had read the enemy, counted them, sectored them. Then he'd hit them where he thought the hitting would yield the best results. There had been no grand dream of obliterating the enemy from this landscape. Bolan was a realist. He did not rely on miracles. He knew that a one-man army had its limitations. Given enough time, sure, a guy who knew his business could eventually put the Detroit mob out of business. That was the hooker, though. There was not that much *time* on earth left at Bolan's disposal—certainly not that much time left in Detroit. His whole success thus far had been built upon commando tactics. Invade the enemy with great force, raise all the hell possible, then withdraw—and all of it to the cadence count, on tight numbers, moving swiftly and never letting down until withdrawal was complete. Any deviation from that timetable could be disastrous.

The strike at Detroit had been carefully planned along those very lines. The timing could not have been better. He'd caught them mobbed into a business conference, and he'd struck them there. He'd sent them in squalling and disorganized retreat, and he'd served notice on their "friends" that doing business with the mob could be hazardous. Also, he would have brought their damned hard-site down and left the rubble for them to contemplate—and the Detroit hit would have been worth it for that alone. Their God-complex would have been shaken, if nothing else.

But, sure, *things* were in the saddle at Detroit.

Here sat the commando force, twelve hours off its numbers, completely derailed from the original mission, contemplating the end of the game.

Leo Turrin had not been exaggerating the situation. Bolan's recon had yielded the same intelligence. *Death* was watching him. And all he could do was *watch* her *back*.

Well . . . not quite. He was still on the offensive. The game had changed a bit, sure, but the enemy was still the enemy, and Bolan was still Bolan—and he had not been ridden beneath the waves of blood river yet.

The dictates of an impersonal war had yielded to a strongly personal responsibility. Okay, call it by its true name: duty. Bolan had a duty to perform for a couple of daughters of Eve—and, in the face of that duty, he could gaze back at Death and spit in her eye.

Could, hell.

He *had* to.

Any other course of action or inaction would amount to nothing more than a *contempt* for *life*.

Things were *always* in the saddle. The ride had something to do with that same cosmic magic that Bolan had contemplated an eternity or so ago with Toby Ranger in his arms. A guy could honor the ride—and gallop off into his own destiny—or he could try to throw the rider and slink back to a safe stable.

Eugene O'Neill once had a very similar thought.

136

"Contentment is a warm sty for eaters and sleep-ers."

It had been a long time since Mack Bolan had known contentment. He did not seek it now.

He would ride the good ride, wherever it might lead.

Let *Death* watch.

The Executioner was saddled and ready.

"Pete's sake!" Toby exclaimed. "This blooming truck is a rolling arsenal."

"Right, and she's going along for the ride," Bolan replied. "I want you to use the vehicle I came in. It's hot, so be careful."

"Great," she said. "With everything else, all I need now is to get caught with a stolen car."

"Worse," he said, smiling. "It's a police car. And they're onto me. So stay off the radio. I be-lieve they're rolling around with direction fin-ders."

Toby's eyes were wide, wondering. "You are the *damnedest . . .*"

Bolan laughed softly and told her, "I want you to run a little diversion for me." He pulled her into the van section and placed her in front of a large city map that was taped to the wall. His fin-ger traced the line marking the division between Wayne and Macomb Counties at the northern boundary of Grosse Pointe Woods, then circled a specific point.

"That's where?" she asked.

"That's where. This street, this block."

"What is that?"

He said quietly, "Look again."

137

"Well, it's just . . ." Her breath drew in sharply. "What are those red numbers? The house numbering system?"

"Right."

She said, "Fourteen-ninety."

"Uh huh. And the house we're interested in carries the number 1492. Second house on the right, running north."

"Well, I'll be . . ."

Bolan said, "Strange, isn't it?"

"I figured the number had to do with—it couldn't be a coincidence. Could it?"

He sighed and squeezed her shoulders. "I decided a long time ago, Toby. There's no such thing as coincidence in this magic-ridden old world. The man who lives at 1492 is, I think, our key to Georgette. I need to get in there and find out for sure."

"He's home now?"

Bolan nodded. "Holed up is the word. Hasn't budged out of there all day."

"So what are we waiting for?"

"The house is staked out. Two cars. One just north and across from the house, another around the corner and down the side street about a half-block east."

Toby was squinting at the map in the semidarkness.

Bolan flipped on a battery-powered lantern.

She said, "Okay, I see it. What do you want me to do?"

"I want you to drive that hot car in there."

"Oh, wow. Right up to the house, eh?"

"Yeah. But do it cute. Tie something about your head so that blonde hair doesn't show. Don't give them a good look at you. Turn off your headlamps as you're approaching, and leave them off. Roll quietly into the driveway and just sit there."

"What kind of driveway?"

"Crescent, about fifty feet long, circling in off the road."

She sighed. "Roll in and just sit there."

"Right."

"How long?"

"Long enough to get me quietly inside." He tapped the map. "I'll be coming in from back here. I'll leave the war wagon here and go on by foot. From the time you turn onto that street, I'll need about two minutes. So you've got to cute it for at least that long."

"Okay. I can do that. You want me to roll in past the side street stake-out."

"Right. I want them both to see you."

"You want them to *catch* me."

He squeezed her shoulders again. "I don't want them to *shoot* you, Toby. When they begin closing, the game is up. There's an element of risk. This is a Mad Dog alert."

"Yes, I know," she murmured.

"When they close, call out to them. Let them have a good look at you. From then on, it's your game. I guess you know the best way to play it."

"Sure," she said, still staring at the map.

He said, "Okay. Let's move."

"Mack . . ."

"Yeah?"

"Do you believe there's any chance that Georgette—that she—could she be in that house, alive?"

He told her, "The world is full of magic, Toby."

"Yes, I—okay, let's go."

She whirled and grabbed him, arms encircling his neck, lips at his ear. "Stay alive," she whispered.

"Name of the game," he muttered lightly.

"If Georgette is already lost—if she's—it's not a smart trade, Captain Cocky. Don't bury yourself in her grave."

"Who's cocky?" he quietly replied. "If you have a better plan, I'm all ears."

"It's a long shot, isn't it."

"In this game, Toby, they all are. You know that."

"Sure. Sure. Well . . ."

He sighed and asked her, "You're not still dreaming of green pastures?"

She shivered, "Why not? I still belong to the human race."

"Right," he said. "That's why we have to get moving, Toby."

"Thanks for reminding me." She released him, swiped angrily at moist cheeks, and stepped outside.

Night had fallen. The atmosphere was still, oppressive, brooding.

Bolan followed her out, and they synchronized watches, all taut business once again. "Follow me to the neighborhood," he instructed her. "Stay about a block behind, but keep me in sight. I'll start my move two blocks west of target. You go it alone from that point, and you hit that drive precisely on the hour."

"Will do," she murmured. Then: "How and where do we rejoin?"

He said, "You kidding? You expect to talk your way clear?"

She said, "They have to catch me first."

Bolan stepped back and growled, "It's scrubbed."

"Oh, damn it! Down, Captain Gruff. I won't do anything dumb. But don't underestimate the jaw power of a lady fed. Now, where do we rejoin?"

He told her, in a flat and level tone, "Toby, it's a Mad Dog. Don't give them any reason whatever to start jerking triggers."

"How about the apartment? Okay?"

She was giving him the winsome smile, working him—and he knew it. He bunched his shoulders, growled something unintelligible, then said, "Okay. It's your game, too, Toby. The apartment's okay. Just don't bring a flock of badges with you."

"Just get yourself back there," she growled in the same harsh tone.

He lifted her off her feet, very solemnly kissed her, put her down, spun her around, and sent her off with a gentle slap on the bottom.

Then he climbed into the war wagon and went rolling into the jungle. It was a human jungle, the worst kind of all, filled with cannibals and headhunters of every stripe and persuasion, patrolled by game wardens with ready guns who knew all the drops and preserves and poachers—and, yeah, at such times even Mack Bolan gave a thought or two to greener pastures.

But, he knew, green pastures were for the dead. Warm sties and safe stables were no place to live the worthy life. There was no cosmic sprawl in such places, no magic worth pursuing.

Bolan's destiny lay in that uncertain sprawl that some men called *hell*. Bolan called it *life*. And he would *live* it, to the final gasp.

19: BAGGED

"Lee!"

"Yeah."

"A slow roller, coming west. Wait . . . yeah. Can't make the occupant but . . . it's a loner. The car looks . . . whup! Hang on! That's our bogey!"

"Okay, sit tight! Hold station!"

"Right! Passing me now. Still can't make—but that's it, that's our car!"

"Okay. I have him in sight. What's he doing?"

"Holding at the intersection. Can't make up his mind. Maybe he's sniffed us."

"Sit tight! Harvey's passing the word to roving leader. Just sit, damn it!"

"We're sitting. There he goes! Coming at you!"

"I have him. Start your move."

"We're moving, man!"

"Slowly, slowly—hold it! He's stopped again!"

"Damn damn *damn!*"

"Casing it. Might decide to go on around. Hold where you are."

"Get the rovers over here, damn it!"

"They're moving. So's our man, now. Okay, come on around. Seal his behind!"

"Sealed! How soon will rover be here?"

"They're on the shore drive and hotting it! Keep that plug in! Okay . . . okay . . . yeah. This is it! Killed his lights. There he goes! Pulled right into the damned driveway! I've lost him! How's your angle?"

"No good. Trees blocking."

"We're moving in on foot. Passing radio to you. Guard channel delta sub one. Keep rovers advised!"

"Right! Watch yourselves!"

It was a large room, a combination for sleeping and working. Double French doors opened onto a small balcony overlooking the front. A small sitting area near there. Gleaming mahogany desk at one wall, king-sized bed against the other. Dressing table, walk-in wardrobe—behind there a large bath, door open, lights on.

The wall behind the desk was ornamented with numerous framed photographs, each depicting the master of the manse in an intimate setting with some "great man."

Cassiopea with the vice-president, autographed "to Cass, with warmest appreciation."

Cassiopea with a familar European statesman, autographed "to my dear friend Cass, without whom we would be diminished."

Cassiopea with a robed and bearded Arab chieftain, annotated illegibly in a spidery Eastern scrawl.

Cassiopea with a veteran Hollywood superstar, inscribed simply "to Cass Baby."

And on and on.

Cass Baby was standing at the French doors, peering cautiously through a crack in the heavy draperies.

The guy must have been dressed by some movie director, all the way to smoking jacket and briarwood pipe with a fancily curved stem. Manicured nails reflected the light from the lone lamp in use —a small desk affair—hair dark and glossy, streaked handsomely, meticulously brushed and shaped.

A neat stack of papers and a telephone were the sole adornments of the desk.

Bolan held a marksman's medal at shoulder height and allowed it to fall to the gleaming surface of the desk. It hit with a small clatter.

The guy whirled around, annoyance covering the face for a split second before being shoved aside by fear and wonder.

Darting dark eyes flashed to the metallic object on the desk—flared, then swung rapidly from side to side seeking reassurance—settling finally on the tall man with the icy gaze.

The handsome head cocked and the terrified man crowed: *"Bruce! Harry!"*

"Save it," Bolan suggested coldly. "Bruce and Harry are sleeping off a double Excedrin headache. It's just you and me, Cass Baby."

The guy's mouth opened and closed. He swayed to the desk and sat on the corner, slumping across

145

it. Perspiration began to appear on the forehead and upper lip. He was transfixed by the medal of death.

"I know what that is," he declared in a shaky voice.

"Then you know who I am."

Cassiopea nodded his head as though it were too heavy to be moved. He said, in a voice gaining control, "Yes. I know you. But I cannot understand why you are here. What can I possibly do for you?"

"You could die for me, Cass Baby."

The guy was a smoothy, and he was getting his second wind. He came right back at Bolan without blinking. "That makes no sense whatever. I've been following your, uh, crusade with great interest. I understand your motivations. Sympathize with them. And let me assure you, Bolan, I have no part in them."

Bolan hit him—flat of the hand—a haymaker from the knees, connecting that handsomely chiseled jawline with a splat that echoed around the room. Cassiopea spun off the desk to land on hands and knees, against the wall.

Bolan went to the windows and looked down. Toby was just pulling into the drive.

Cass Baby was hauling himself upright, both hands groping at the desk, shaking his head as though trying to clear it of bothersome foreign matter.

Bolan allowed him to get to the desk drawer and open it before springing the Belle. She chugged once and spat destruction into the wood of the drawer.

Cassiopea flung himself away from there, bounced off the wall once again, then made a lurching run for the open door.

The Beretta sighed twice more. A pair of streakers won the footrace, punching the door with a fast and loud one-two, slamming it shut in Cass Baby's face.

He turned about in full wilt, defeated now by his own trembling legs, crumbling to a kneeling position, arms raised in terrified supplication. *"God's sake, man! Why are you playing with me?"*

The guy wanted logic in a world of lunacy.

"It's your game, guy," the ice man told him. "Just tell me when you're through playing."

It was the moment of final truth for Bobby Cassiopea. Pulsing into that climactic heartbeat—gazing, perhaps for the first time, into what Bolan called the "cosmic sprawl"—a man knows when the masquerade is ended, the posturing and swaggering is done, the party is over. With *Death* gazing upon him, every man sees the end of dreams. All of the maybes and might-have-beens have run out of time, and the man sits alone with precisely what he has become, no more and no less, the savings account of the soul at full maturity.

And Bobby Cassiopea's soul was, obviously, sweating blood.

He was bagged, and he knew it.

20: BOUGHT

Toby swung the car into the drive and glided to the portico with power off, fluffing out her hair and damning herself almost immediately. She should have hesitated for a few precious seconds out there at the edge of the drive, playing for every second of indecision and wonderment that could possibly be worked on those watchers out there.

She heard the mechanical action of a car door and then feet moving swiftly along the pavement, and she damned herself again.

They were closing on foot.

A minute and forty seconds. *That was all she had given him!*

The difference between life and death was often a matter of a split second!

Good God, what had she done?

She leapt from the car and ran to the center of the small lawn, wild thoughts tearing at her.

The *slap slap* of cautiously hurrying shoe leather galvanized her and sent her mind leaping. They were advancing along the drive.

She tripped over something on the lawn, bent to peer at it through the darkness, and knew immediately what she had to do. She snatched the thing up and hurled it toward the street with all her might.

It was a piece of a broken lawn ornament, a cement dish or something, shaped like a discus. The heavy object hit the pavement with a crash and skittered loudly on, veritably thundering through the quietness of that tense moment.

The footfalls ceased abruptly and a startled voice quietly called, "What the hell!"

"On the street!" another man barked in a hoarse whisper.

Heavy bodies floundered into dense shrubs.

Toby ran back to the vehicle, dived in, started the engine, floored the gas pedal, and jammed the gearshift into driving range. The car roared from beneath the portico as though shot from a catapult, door open and swinging shut with a crash as momentum overtook it.

Headlamps flared, showing her the way in a tire-screaming swerve. She momentarily lost pavement and spun into soft turf, fishtailed, leapt back with another loud shriek from protesting rubber, hit the end of the drive at full pedal—swerving again, fishtailing down the street and struggling for stability.

At the rear edge of pulsating consciousness came the *ba-loom* of a shotgun and then another mixed with the rapid-fire banging of a pistol. The window behind her disintegrated, and something like an icepick punching through a tin can was playing upon the rear of the car.

Headlamps flared to the rear as a vehicle roared into pursuit.

She was moving strongly and eating pavement at a flat 80 mph as the first intersection north leapt into her probing headlights and something very ominous swept across her line of sight. It was a procession of vehicles, moving fast, wheeling through that intersection and coming her way.

And, in the lead, was a heavy armored riot car, beacon twirling, hunching into a fast slowdown and crabbing slowly, slowly, directly across her line of travel.

"Dumb!" she screamed at the night. "Dumb dumb dumb!"

But she'd given the man his two minutes. And, perhaps, considerably more than that.

"Damn it, just *damn it!*"

At that very moment a greatly disturbed Mack Bolan was dragging an even more disturbed "playboy of the western financial world" down the stairs and out the rear of the house—dragging him by the tail of his fancy silk smoking jacket, flat on his butt and wailing to an audience under the stars.

Bolan had heard the commotion out front, of course—and he knew, he knew. The greater sounds of the night were now swirling about the entire neighborhood—and they could have but one reading.

He curled both hands into the silk at Cass

Baby's throat and shook him like a panther would shake his catch. The normally icy tones were heated with the rage of hopeless frustration as he told the quivering blubber before him, "The cost has gone too high, guy. For a miserable slaver—a pimp at the court of kings, you lousy . . ."

"*God's sake, get it over with!*" Cassiopea screamed.

"So Sal gave her a punishment to fit the crime, eh?" Bolan raged on. "I'm giving you the same, guy!"

He ripped the pants off the guy and flung him to the grass flat on his back, pinning him there with a foot on the throat while he sprang the wicked stiletto.

The guy gurgled, "What? *What?* No, God, no—*not that!*"

"What's wrong, Eunuch Baby? Doesn't the punishment fit?"

"My God, I don't think she's dead! I'm sure she's not! Just look where I told you. God, *don't* do *this!*"

Bolan buried the stilletto into the ground between the guy's quivering legs. "Next time," he promised, "your stinking sperm will be spilling. If you've lied to me, guy . . . this is your last chance to fix it."

"I swear! *Swear!*"

Bolan left Cass Baby there, half-swooning and stewing in his own bitter juices.

It was no fun baiting a guy that way. Necessary, sure, but not fun. Necessary because the truth had suddenly become so damned important. And Bolan's own rage at the unhappy turn of events out front made the baiting only about half sham. And he was at least 99% certain that he'd squeezed the bleeding truth from the guy.

But that "victory" was not so sweet. Not at all sweet. As Toby had said, during those last moments when they were together, the goal may not be worthy of the cost of the search.

A bag of bones did not a victory make.

And a snappy lady fed who just damn it had to think for herself had obviously decided to pay the supreme price.

If she had . . . damn it, if she had . . .

Yeah. Men could cry, too.

21: SOLD

Holzer had been en route home for a quick clean-up, a bite of chow, maybe even a brief nap, when he intercepted the contact alert from Strike 8.

It had been a damned long day, with strain enough during the past eight hours alone to wring a guy dry.

He had been up with this case for almost twenty hours—but the flash from Grosse Pointe Woods was like a magic wand waved above his head.

He felt as giddy as a teen-ager chasing a fire truck when he sighted the task force beating it along the shore drive—downright exultant when he saw them take the turn up Vernier.

This was *his* territory, by damn—he knew a better and quicker way that should put him on the scene a couple of ticks ahead of the pack.

He flashed on past the Grosse Pointe Yacht Club and took a death-defying turn onto Hawthorne, letting out his siren and running with lady luck in a balls-out sprint to Marter, then screaming north into the stretch for Yorktown Parkway.

Straightening into the parkway, he killed the screamer and went it on beacon alone. He damn near creamed a putt-putting Volkswagen at the first intersection, immediately thereafter shakily deciding to sacrifice a bit of speed in the interest of survival. Sure as hell he wanted to at least *be there* for the wrap-up of this case.

As he would later recall, that slowdown was primarily responsible for the weird things that followed.

Holzer was approaching the scene on a westerly course. The destroyer force *should* have been pounding northward from Vernier on a right-angle course to his. But, obviously, they had made a circle-around for some tactical reason, and now he could see them swinging onto the parkway just ahead to run westerly along his same approach . . . and leading him by a good two hundred yards.

So Holzer swung south, then west again, fuming over being beat out in his own backyard and damned if he would run up their tails.

Another spine-tingling turn and he was now running northward, approaching the scene on the path that had apparently been rejected by the roving detail.

He did not have their tac channel on his radio and therefore could not understand the play.

All he could do now was lose the race.

But he heard the double *ba-loom* of a riot gun and other firing far ahead, and he was close enough to see that plunging vehicle careening into

154

the trap—and now he understood the maneuvers of the Tac Force—damn it—just a flash too late, he understood them.

Another vehicle had been parked broadside in the street just beyond the intersection. It was now wheeling about in hot pursuit of the fleeing vehicle.

Holzer could not brake his charge from ninety to zip in the time required to avoid running up on the chase vehicle, but he gave it the old college try, suddenly painfully aware that he was interfering with a closely coordinated trap set.

He hit brakes and wheel together and locked them in, spinning dizzily for a moment, then recovering to careen into the intersection and plunge eastward along the side street.

Well, almost.

His front wheels jumped the curb, and he plowed through shrubs and saplings for about two hundred feet before wrenching loose and going into a skid toward the other side.

He hit a fence over there, and his bumper must have caught on something immovable. It popped him around like the snap of a whip, pushing him ino a sidewise skid that quickly became a roll, and Holzer in his seat strap inanely thought of those kid days at the fair and the rollo-plane when he chucked up meatballs and spaghetti in a spray onto the onlookers below—at the same moment wondering if that was to be his dying thought, the sole flashback of a life he had thought so memorable . . . what a hell of a way to go.

He blacked out. For how long, he could not guess—probably no more than a matter of seconds. He came out of it with the awareness of flames strong in his consciousness and mixed with the stark realization that he was pinned immobile in a collapsed vehicle that could blow sky high at any moment.

In the licking of flames he saw a devil dancing in the street just outside—but then he immediately decided that this was merely another "death flashback." It was not a devil dancing.

It was Mack Bolan, that same face that had grinned at him so winningly and framed the words: "Let's see, it's John Holzer, isn't it?"

Yeah, and even at that it was better than meatballs and spaghetti in upchuck.

But the vision was not holding to the script. What it was saying was, "Don't move. Stay calm. I'll get you out."

Shit! *No flashback!*"

The goddamn guy was out there, *in the flesh.*

Holzer tried his own mouth and found it working. And, of course, it came up with something appropriately stupid. "How'd you get here so quick, Stryker?"

"Just happened along," the big, cool bastard replied. "Listen now. It's a bad situation. The windshield has come down on you. There's a jagged edge poised right at your jugular vein. I can't move it. The roof is buckled in. The gas tank could go any minute. If I raise that roof, you're liable to get it in the neck. If I don't raise it, you're sure to either fry or fly. So I've got to raise it. Soon as you can get your hands free, protect your throat all you can."

"Got you," Holzer said, surprising himself with

156

his own detachment. "How're you going to raise it?"

"The only way I know," the guy said.

And then he was in there with Holzer, on hands and knees in that wreckage. Holzer could see the veins popping in the guy's neck, could almost *feel* the surge of vital juices flowing into challenged muscles as the guy groaned and strained to straighten himself.

"Watch it!" the guy grunted.

And then John Holzer felt the impossible occurring, the roof moving off of him, an arm loosening —and the guy strained on.

"It's coming," Holzer whispered. "Hold it . . . wait! . . . my throat—*ungh*—okay, got it. Shit, man, let's go."

Thinking back on it, Holzer realized what a fantastic feat it had been; at the moment it seemed as easy as smoothing a piece of rumpled Reynold's Wrap.

Suddenly the guy had him by the armpits, tugging him loose, pulling him free, grunting and damning and dragging in a mad frenzy—and then it went, the gas tank.

The heat from that towering fireball singed the hairs of Holzer's head, and all he could do was lie there and grunt, aware of being alive and thankful.

A hoarse voice close to his ear whispered, "Spit in her eye, Holzer."

The message did not register at first; he was transfixed by the staggering proximity and undeniable majesty of flaming death. When he did turn groggy eyes toward he sound of that voice, here was no one there.

He began crawling, and he called out, "Stryker! Are you okay? *Stryker!*"

That was when the sergeant from East Detroit came running up. "Oh, Jesus!" the cop yelled. "Is anybody *in* there?"

"Just John Holzer," Holzer replied. "I'll be in there for the rest of my life, amen."

"Who was that you were yelling for? Who was with you?"

Holzer struggled to his feet, surprised that he could stand. His hands were cut where he had grabbed the shattered windshield—but the damage was negligible and seemed to be his only visible injury.

"Who was with you?" the East Detroit cop yelled again.

"God," Holzer mumbled. "*God* was with me, man."

22: FULFILLED

Dumb? Dumb screaming *providence*, that's what it was!

She had hesitated for one frozen moment, the image of Bolan strong upon her peaking perceptions of this possibly final glimpse of life—hesitated . . . then again plunged the accelerator to full stomp and leaned into the wheel with everything she had.

The car leapt the curb at full throttle, becoming airborne momentarily, the rear end heeling over and striking the front corner of the armored vehicle, then swinging wildly out of that impact—pivoting while poised on front wheels only, the transmission freed and whining in full rev.

Then the rear wheels slammed into soft lawn and the wild gallop resumed, totally out of control now, goaded on by the unrelenting pressure of a tiny foot upon a willing accelerator—a mustang snorting its defiance against entrapment, rearing and pawing the earth in a plunging circle toward certain doom.

She was into the house before she saw it, crashing through boards and glass and plaster, pushing couches and chairs and draperies ahead—and, sure, it was like a mad dream of a crazy women's libber—FUCK HOUSEWORK in ten-foot flaming letters on a poster no artist could draw.

She briefly experienced the sensation of flight and knew that she had been flung from the belly of the arrested beast.

And she found herself in bed beside a startled elderly man who kept croaking, "What? What? What?"

Toby muttered, "You're dreaming, go back to sleep."

Her back hurt, and as she scrambled away from there, she felt like an oversized Raggedy Ann—all flopping legs and arms—but she seemed to be moving fairly well, so she kept going.

Through the shattered wall she could see cops in riot togs moving cautiously forward, while another cop, out of her range of vision, was insisting, "A *woman*, I'm telling you. Or a blond hippy. I saw the occupant clear as . . ."

Toby was moving swiftly in the opposite direction, giving not a damn about how clearly the officer had seen her.

She let herself out the back door and ran across the yard, hurtled a low fence, dashing through the adjoining property and emerging on the next street east at full flight.

She did not stop running unil she saw the bulk of that familiar vehicle parked in the alleyway several blocks along, though her belly was busting and her lungs were afire.

Her first reaction to sighting the war wagon was one of elation, but that disappeared under the immediate onslaught of a new anxiety.

Why was it still there?

He should have been miles away by now!

She slowed to a walk, clutching tortured sides in crossed arms and struggling for breath, and when she reached the vehicle she crumbled to the ground and wailed, "Well, damn it, just damn it!"

A gruff voice from the darkness commanded, "Off your tail, and on your feet, partner."

Yeah, sure, it was her guy—in one piece but slightly frayed here and there—a tail burnt off his coat and blood on his hands, but, God, what a big, beautiful bastard he was.

"What kept you, Captain Tortoise?" she panted. "That was a hell of a long two minutes!"

He picked her up and carried her into the van, placed her on the bunk, and tenderly inspected her parts.

"Damn it, Toby," he said solemnly. "Just damn it."

"I'm all present and accounted for, sir. Aren't I?"

"You sure are," he said.

Yes, she sure was. But the warrior wasn't.

"Captain Tearful!" she cried in genuine surprise and flowing concern, viewing his face clearly for the first time since the reunion—and she pulled the man's head onto her breast and held him there.

"Go ahead," she crooned. "Let it out, let it go."

161

"Can't," he muttered in a choked voice. "Guess I'm just not man enough yet."

Even so, it was cosmic magic—of a different sort. And Toby the Lady Fed had never felt more a woman.

23: PROMISED

Toby drove while Bolan changed into combat rig. They talked through the opening between cab and van.

"How were things in 1492?" she inquired with forced lightness.

"Enlightening," he replied. "And ominous."

"Well, how about giving a girl some ominous enlightenment."

"If I tell you at all, Toby, I have to tell it all. I don't know how to color it."

She cast a dark glance over her shoulder. "I've never asked you for colors."

He cinched up the black suit and gave it to her straight. "Crazy Sal sentenced Georgette to fifty days in the chamber."

"The chamber? What's that?"

"The guy back there claims he doesn't know any more than that. And maybe he doesn't. If it's what I think."

163

"Okay, what do you think it is?"

"Let me tell you the other first. The guy at 1492 is a big international money front for the Detroit mob. He handles literally hundreds of millions of dollars a year—some of it mere trading paper, but quite a bit in cool black cash. The entire movement is half legit, half business as usual for the boys. And that last half covers all the sins. If you have the cannibal instinct, you know, you can eat a lot of people in the legitimate business world."

"And God knows," Toby sniffed, "even the straight ones are cannibal enough."

"What a difference, though," Bolan said. "Sure big money carries all sorts of filth with it regardless of who's handling it, but these mob people have their own disinctive flair for hot rape. And their own cute games. Like 1492, case in point. This guy isn't satisifed to simply influence the bouncing bucks with free sex. He likes to capture them with a club. The club, of course, being that same free sex, only it turns out to be expensive as hell. You were right about the party girl jet set. A street-corner hooker is Saint Joan by comparison with these kids. The 1492 girls are cannibals of a different stripe, and the power they carry between their thighs is awesome to contemplate—when you know the international figures they're playing hotsy with. Of course, the mob can't afford to let that kind of power become independent or competitive. They need to own these girls, own their very souls."

"You're talking about industrial blackmail."

"With a variation or two, yeah. Political blackmail, also. Which is why 1492 handles soul recruiting the way it does. They take the girls with a club, too. Corrupt them with terror and shame and everything else they can lay on them, then send them into the jungle to bring home some hard-to-get stocks, or a new company, or whatever else is hot in the marketplaces at the moment—maybe even a small, but developing, nation here and there."

"I know the routine," Toby reported, tight-lipped. "What's that *chamber?*"

Bolan replied, "Only my gut knows for sure. I believe I can tell you this much. Georgette has been held up as some sort of object lesson to new recruits. They parade the new souls through this 'chamber' to show what could happen to *them* if they ever develop cute ideas about not playing ball with their new masters."

Toby shuddered. She whispered, "Oh, my God."

Bolan said, "Yeah. A chamber of horrors. Have you ever seen a turkey, Toby?"

"I've heard of them," she replied shakily. "Are you saying that Georgette . . . ?"

"You said no colors," Bolan muttered. "And that's what my gut is telling me about Georgette."

"Oh, my God."

"Yeah." He buckled on the automag and tested the action.

"Did you say for *fifty days?*"

"That's the story."

"But how could they . . . ?" Toby shuddered again. "How could anyone *take* it that long?"

"Let's hope she couldn't, Toby. Pray that she's long dead."

"My God, my God."

He slithered into the Beretta rig, sprung her twice, checked the clip, secured Whispering Death.

"Where are we going?"

"You know the place."

"I do?"

He raised the lid of a munitions chest and began selecting weapons for the hunt.

"Do I?" she repeated.

"You said it held some secrets. I believe it does."

"You can't hit that place again so soon!" Toby cried. "It would be crazy suicide!"

"Maybe so. But there's more than one route to suicide, Toby. I can't walk away from this one."

"But not if she's dead already! It would be senseless, wasteful!"

Bolan closed the chest and drummed his fingers on the lid.

Toby pulled the war wagon to the curb and turned to him with a tortured gaze.

He asked her quietly, "Are you ready to write her off, Toby?"

She just stared at him.

He said, "There are ways of keeping people alive . . . through almost anything. These people have turkey doctors who—"

"Oh, shut up!" Toby screamed.

"Did you ever read the Nuremberg reports on the surgical techniques used by the Nazi lunatics? Do you *know* what a skilled surgeon without a soul can *do* to a living body—and keep it living? Have you ever—?"

"*Shut up! Just shut up!*"

"Let's roll, partner."

She mauled her lower lip between grinding teeth, realizing the pain only when she tasted blood, then told the man, "Not for my sake, Captain Gallant. This one is not for me. She's dead and I know it. You know it, too. So this one is not for Toby."

"Call it for me, then," Bolan muttered. "And roll this goddamned hearse. Now!"

She rolled it, reluctantly, and Bolan resumed his preparations for war.

A moment later she told him, "Okay. But I'm going in with you."

"The hell you are."

Tears were streaming down her face, diluting the blood at her lips. She said, "And just when I was getting to really like you."

"Stop thinking, Toby. Just drive."

"I've felt more alive today than I ever have. I don't want it to end, Captain Honey. I just can't stand to lose it now. Not *now*."

He told her, "You can't lose something you've never owned, Toby."

"Thanks; that hurt like hell. I don't want to *own* you."

"I didn't mean me."

"Oh hell, Mack! What are we *doing*? What's the sense of all this? God, tell me God, what are we *doing*?"

"Living, Toby. We're just living. Largely."

"I'll settle for *small*."

"No, you wouldn't. Tell you what, though. I'll share an R&R with you. After this. We'll take a few days off from living, and we'll just graze in green pastures until we've both had a bellyful. Okay?"

She smiled through tears and told him, "That's a cheap promise. From a dead man."

He said, "I'm not dead yet."

"Green pastures, eh? Okay. Okay."

But the green, green hills of home seemed terribly remote, at that moment, to the somber man in black.

It was a cheap promise, sure.

Toby called back to him, "We're getting close. What's the plan? Quiet entry?"

He glanced outside to orient himself, then replied, "No. Not for this one, Toby. Pull into the next street west, and stop."

For this one, no. No quiet entry.

Charley Fever would be expecting it, and all the quiet ways would be under heavy patrol.

This one would be a hit—a hard swing to the solar plexus—thunder and lightning and hell on the hoof.

And let *Death* pick up her pieces where she would.

24: DEAD

A smoke cannister whizzed over the wall directly between the twin gatehouses at SCYC and fell
to the lawn, spewing a dense black cloud, followed
immediately by another and then another—each
spaced about a hundred feet apart.

The gate captain bellowed an anguished alarm
and hit the double-lock, while another guard fum-
bled with a walky-talky radio.

Then a gray van with a canvas satchel draped
across the grill leapt out of the shadows of the ac-
cess road and charged along the fifty-foot approach to the chute, steadily gaining speed.

A panicky guard on the catwalk connecting the
two gates opened fire on the vehicle with a chatter
gun. The windshield shattered, but the truck bore
on.

Someone screamed, *"Look out!"*

Then it hit, dead center on the outer gate, blowing through with a fanastic explosion that shook the night all over those grounds.

A wall of the main gatehouse promptly disintegrated. The catwalk tilted, cracked, then collapsed into the chute.

And that was not all.

The demolished van skittered on, wedging itself into the narrow chute halfway between the two gates. A second explosion triggered itself seconds after the catwalk fell in, and this one outdid the first by several points on the Richter scale. Debris from both gatehouses flew in an almost horizontal movement in a farflung pattern across those bedeviled grounds as desperate voices screamed into the night.

While the displaced pieces were settling, a solitary figure in combat black stalked across the no-man's-land and calmly walked into hell.

As he moved through the shattered area, he pulled a gas mask into place and heaved another smoke cannister far ahead.

He bore a military pack on both chest and back. The massive head weapon, a .44 magnum autoloader, occupied prime position in the right hand. The left held a hand grenade—dead-man-armed with five seconds of fuse.

A pistol yapped at him from the left flank. Without breaking stride he squeezed off two thunderous retorts from the automag—and the yapping abruptly ceased.

He stepped into the smoke and guided his progress with one foot moving along turf, the other scraping paved drive. He was a pack mule, and it was necessary that he move like one. The weight upon those feet was nearly double the usual.

The night was dead, breezeless, unreal, as viewed through the visor of the mask and choked with the heavy atmosphere of chemically produced smoke.

Shadowy figures were running blindly and wheezing in all directions around him.

The guy had found his bullhorn again and was exhorting the troops from some place safely removed.

Bolan the Mule plodded on, pausing only to grip the mag between firm teeth now and then while he heaved another ration of smoke—and he continued thusly, unmolested, all the way to the parking area beside the house.

A fire team with wet towels at their faces occupied the small porch at the side entrance, five of them jammed onto that small oasis of relatively unpolluted atomosphere.

The sighting was instantaneous on both sides.

A volley of reactively hasty fire crackled into the charged environment of doom as Bolan merged back with the smoke. His left arm executed a half-circle in a softball pitch.

The grenade dropped into the pile-up and the HE pummeled the clear zone and scattered smoking bodies in every direction. One of the victims was afire with flames leaping up his back; he rose to hands and knees then pitched forward without a sound.

Bolan sent him a .44 mercy round just to make sure, then resumed the assault plan.

He hit the windows at both levels with a combination of smoke and HE, methodically working his

171

way around the big house while people in there stampeded and screamed for assistance from hired guns who had apparently lost all taste for the wages of war. Guys were running all over the grounds and yelling, yet the direct challenges to the tall man in executioner black were scattered and brief. The big, rolling booms of the automag seldom competed with the more devastating thunder of high explosives that continually puffed and rocked and swayed that hellhouse.

The artificial smoke had become an unnecessary factor by the time Bolan's chestpack gaped empty and limp.

The shattered building was shooting flames and billowing honest smoke from every opening—and there were numerous new ones. Guys were leaping from second-story windows and lying about, groaning, everywhere.

Bolan shed the useless pack and invaded the pandemonium, moving swiftly and surely to the only area that could possibly produce the results he sought from this strike.

He found it where he thought he would—in the sub-basement—he was chilled by the knowledge that he had stood less than two paces from *truth* on his last trip into here.

Yeah, Toby, the joint held secrets.

The hidden door creaked open to his expert touch, and he found himself in a small lounge area —not much larger than an ordinary bathroom. A tattered chair shared the space with a small table upon which rested a double hotplate and a stained coffee pot, an open box of Baby Ruth candy bars, and a six-pack of Dr. Pepper.

172

Bolan had actually looked into there the night before, found it empty, and went on.

It was not empty now.

A fat ghoul was standing stiffly against the far wall, staring at the visiting apparition with a resigned snarl.

Yeah, Bolan thought, *small damned underworld!*

It was the turkey doctor whom Bolan had encountered so briefly, yet so traumatically, on that back door of hell in central Jersey. He knew the guy only as "Sal," and even that was too much knowledge for Mack Bolan to stomach.

He removed the gas mask and told the fat man, "Two Crazy Sals under one roof is too much for my belly."

"There was but one *crazy* Sal," the guy said haughtily. "I am not programmed by ridiculous emotions."

The smell of Auschwitz and Buchenwald hung heavy in the air between them. Bolan had to fight his trigger finger to keep it cool.

"Spring the door," he commanded icily. "And stand aside."

"Forgive me for not understanding that instruction," said the spirit of scientific savagery.

Bolan helped along the understanding. He shot Fat Sal at the arch of heavy thighs with a 240-grain chunk of nonsurgical steel. The guy screamed and grabbed and fell forward onto his knees, clutching hands instantly dyed red, eyes wild with understanding now.

"How's the perspective from down there, Sal?" Bolan asked soberly. "That's just tab one, spelled

173

Bruno." He kicked the guy out of his path, and the turkey doctor fell onto his side, legs still doubled, and lay there grunting.

Bolan found the springset on his own and opened the trick door, steeled himself, then stepped into the Dark Ages.

A chamber of horrors, yeah. Complete with candelabra and sacrificial altar. Low ceiling, dank cement walls, the smell of mold and mildew surpassed only by that other odor—that *turkey smell* that chased Bolan's dreams down blood river and haunted his wakeful strolls across hell's back acres.

It was a long, narrow room—dominated by the raised surgical table at the center. A series of eight-by-ten glossy photos lined the wall on one side, telling the graphic story of the shredding of a sentient being in grisly, step-by-step detail, each one carefully dated to preserve he continuity of the crime, each one a picture of the same pitiful wreck who now lay upon that dreadful table with the candelabraum at her head.

Crazy Sal sentenced her to fifty days in the chamber.

Fifty enternities was more like it.

A medical device for intravenous feeding stood at the side, connected to the "patient" by a length of clear tubing. It could be used for blood transfusions, as well.

A small table at the other side held hypodermic syringes and vials of liquid.

Oh, how Fat Sal had struggled to keep this one alive and aware. And, God in heaven, *what* an awareness.

She had no feet and no hands.

One eye socket was empty and ghastly in the candleglow.

The other eye was intact but had no lid with which to shutter reality—a reality helped along by an arrangement of mirrors placed for unavoidable viewing.

She also had no breasts.

Where genital labia had been was now a smooth skin graft with a miniature artificial penis to facilitate urination.

A crude "badge" had been carved into her abdomen, glowing redly with raised scar tissue that had been encouraged rather than inhibited.

Yeah! Step by step and day by grisly day the dismemberment of a once beautiful woman had gone relentlessly forward.

Bolan's guts creaked with this firsthand realization, shaking his faith in the worth of the whole human experience.

And—yes, Toby—she was alive . . . breathing with shallow little grunts, defenseless cyclops of an eye roving the face in a mute plea from the bowels of hell itself.

He stood beside her in frozen immobility and groaned, "Canuck, baby—okay, okay."

She tried to speak, but then he saw that she had no tongue and also no teeth—but no speech was really necessary to convey the message from that pleading eye.

He whispered, "Okay. God rest you, Georgette."

The automag roared and the reverberations of that blast sent him reeling out of there.

The lunatic from Hades was still curled into a

knot on the floor. He'd managed to get his pants down and was attempting to stanch the flow of blood with his bare hands.

Bolan stepped over him without a second glance and went on to the larger chamber and through to the main basement. He shrugged off the backpack and carefully removed the contents, shaped the plastics and emplaced the timers, then methodically set the explosives for maximum demolition.

He took a last look around, murmured woodenly, "Rest in peace"—and got out of there.

He was onto the grounds and in clearing atmosphere when the charges detonated. The ground beneath him quivered, and the whole flaming wreck collapsed in on itself, like a giant sand castle gone dry and all its props kicked out.

Bolan was free of excess baggage, now—of the mule-pack variety—but loaded even heavier with burdens of the soul.

Two guys ran upon him in the confused jumble of darkness and promptly wished they hadn't. The automag bellowed massive anger from beneath a face carved in granite death—and the man strode on, oblivious to the shouts and screams and tumult behind him.

He walked unseeing past a crouching Toby Ranger at the edge of nowhere. She trotted along beside him, casting anxious glances into that frozen face but saying nothing, asking nothing.

Finally he halted and dropped to his knees, head falling forward to rest upon the heaving chest, the snout of the .44 pressed into the earth.

She knelt beside him, anxiety now overriding temerity, and she cried, "Are you hurt?"

"No," he whispered. "Not where it shows, Toby."

"My *God*, but you zonked them. I never saw such a . . . Mack—what about—what about . . . ?"

"She's dead," he croaked. "Long dead, Toby." And then he wept.

But not for Georgette Chableu, particularly. He wept for all mankind.

EPILOG

Bolan would not presume to question the internal logic of a universe that he would never understand. He played the game as the numbers fell . . . and what was the sense of shaking one's fist at the heavens?

Death had brought him here to this troubled but improving "City of the Strait" . . . but the death of whom and what?

Death had *watched* as he stumbled blindly across that makeshift stage of human destiny . . . and he'd imagined that he was gazing back at her when in reality he had seen nothing but his own distorted image in search of the role written for him in the stars.

Perhaps a tortured and desperate soul had searched for *him* through that universal maze of living misery, and had led him here to lend it death.

Yeah, maybe.

Death was a *happening*, not a state of being.

He had recovered from the spiritual shock of that ghastly stroll along hell's corridors, and he and his partner were hurrying toward greener pastures when a stolid figure loomed out of the darkness and halted their plunge with a pistol at Bolan's head.

Toby gasped, and Bolan shoved her facedown onto the road as a calm voice inquired, "What took you so long, Stryker?"

The snout of the automag was buried in the guy's belly, Bolan's finger frozen on the trigger by that quietly amiable voice.

He slowly withdrew Big Thunder and holstered him. "You're not the enemy, Holzer," he told the cop. "Either squeeze off or stand aside. There's only one way to take me."

"Take you where?" the guy asked. He sheathed his own pistol. "Sorry about the weapon. Cop can't be too careful on a Mad Dog, you know."

Bolan replied, "Yeah. I know."

"Your, uh, vehicle got destroyed. About the same time and place as mine. Lucky for *me*, eh? I, uh, figured you'd need a replacement."

The tall man in black held out a helping hand to his partner. She scrambled to her feet and stood beside him, glaring into the confrontation with a puzzled frown.

Holzer was asking, "Who was wheeling? The lady here?"

Bolan said, "Could be."

"You've got to be more careful, Stryker. You bear an amazing resemblance to another guy. The whole town is after him. Thought I'd better find you and advise you to vacate the area, very quickly. The, uh, vehicle is just down the street. Keys in. Leave it where it's convenient."

"Thanks," Bolan growled. A hint of a smile played at his lips. "Glad you found me."

"Me, too. Straight-lined you, thinking in a military manner. Figured you might like to know—a place over on the lake shore tumbled down a little while ago, very troublesome place for a cop with territorial pride. With it went three of the meanest old men in Detroit. Plus half of the torpedoes in the area, and half of their boss—a guy called Charley Fever. The other half of Charley, the living half, is enroute to the hospital. Might make it and might not. I'd guess he'd rather not."

"*Men* die easy, Holzer," Bolan growled.

"As opposed to *things*, eh. Guess you're right. Some things you can never touch. Well, a few *things* died tonight, too. Good luck, Stryker."

They touched hands. The man and his lady went on, finding the car where promised.

"Some men die hard," Toby observed, speaking for the first time since the encounter with the law.

"Only if they stay hard," Bolan said. He cranked the engine and put distance between themselves and that hellground back there.

"Does that mean no green pastures?" she asked, small-voiced.

He gripped her hand and showed her a brief smile. "Green pastures are a state of mind, Toby," he said quietly. "I have business in New Orleans and I guess nothing is green down there, not even the grass."

"I see."

"Travel with me part of the way?"

"All the way," she murmured. "Far as you want to take me."

"How about Cloud Nine?"

"I'd settle for Cloud Three or Four. For a day or two."

"Sold," he said, "to the lady with the shiny gold badge."

A tear popped loose as she whispered, "To the memory of Georgie girl. She was a damned good cop, Mack."

Bolan said, "Yeah."

"I'm coming back up here after . . . after . . ."

He said grimly, "Do that. Bust their asses, Toby."

"I intend to."

"Stay hard. Don't give them a goddamned inch. Fight them until they're digesting you, then spit in their bowels. Hit them any way you can, anywhere you can."

She said, "Let me write that down. I'll save it, for your epitaph."

"Do that," he muttered.

She curled an arm into his and whispered, "That's enough shoptalk for now. Let's forget, huh? For a day or two? Just forget?"

Bolan would never forget. Nor would Toby, he knew that. His gaze slid to the rear view mirror, in which was reflected the fading red glimmer above the hellgrouds.

And *Death* gazed back through there . . . smiling, content, sated for the moment. She would rise again, soon, on Bolan's next horizon. He would be ready for her there, too, gazing back upon her.

But, for now, the deathwatch was over.

He snuggled his temporary helpmeet to his side and soberly intoned, "Long live the dead. Forever die the living."

"Down, Captain Coffin, just damn it *down*."

He chuckled, and squeezed her, and they drove into the cosmic sprawl of things to be and things not yet dreamt.

THE "BUTCHER,"
the only man to leave
the Mafia—and live!
A man forever on the run,
unable to trust anyone,
condemned to a life
of constant violence!